I0456430

The End of the Circle

THE END *of the* CIRCLE

stories

WALTER CUMMINS

A Nine Lives
Edition

SERVING HOUSE BOOKS

The End of the Circle

© 2022 by Walter Cummins

All rights reserved

A Nine Lives Edition
Published by Serving House Books
South Orange, New Jersey

www.servinghousebooks.com

ISBN: 978-1-947175-59-4

Library of Congress Control Number: 2022939628

No part of this book may be used or reproduced in any manner whatsoever without the prior written permission of the copyright holder except for brief quotations in critical articles or reviews.

Member of The Independent Book Publishers Association

First Serving House Books Edition 2022

Front Cover: Peter Selgin

Serving House Books Logo: Barry Lereng Wilmont

Originally published by Hopewell Publications Egress Books 2010

To my fellow traveler

Thanks to Tom Kennedy for very valuable advice.

Acknowledgments

"Oxfords," *Virginia Quarterly Review*

"Baggage," *Florida Review*

"The Happy Frenchmen," *Other Voices*

"Stef," *North Atlantic Review*

"What Eamon Did," *Georgetown Review*

"The Beauties of Paris," *Best New Writing 2007*

"Restoring the Castle," *Connecticut Review*

"Awful Advice," *Confrontation*

"Canals," *Portland Review*

"Missing Venice," *Abiko Quarterly*

"Poaching," *Arabesques*

"Freedom," *Princeton Arts Review*

"The End of the Circle," *Bellevue Literary Review*

"Someone Else," *Confrontation*

Contents

OXFORDS

I

Twenty years ago, when they seemed on the verge of a friendship, Henry found Stuart Hartwick tolerable. That is, their wives got on well and Stuart's conversation amused despite his arcane obsessions.

A few years under thirty, Stuart bulked large and portly, formal even at leisure, his white shirts always crisp with starch, his trousers sharply creased, his black slip-on shoes gleaming. His speech, like the rest of him, resounded with precision, each word carefully chosen and articulated. His dark mustache was almost square, and red-veined jowls sagged over tight collars. Unlike Henry, whose brief adulthood had been pinched by academic poverty, he had traveled so widely, imparted such esoteric knowledge of Baltic ferries, Hapsburg palaces, rare wines, and fine silks that Henry found himself content to be an audience.

Their wives had met first, Henry's Elaine and Stuart's Winnie. Young mothers of eight-month-old babies, Joy and Stuart, Jr., nicknamed Tink by Winnie—to Stuart's disdain, the two women found immediate compatibility in talk of formulas, diaper services, and sudden fevers. But Henry couldn't imagine them exchanging a sentence before the babies. Winnie, slow and bland, seemed to have spent her life waiting for the identity that motherhood would bring. Elaine's dark eyes blazed with promise. In fifty years, when their grandchildren were parents, he still would be discovering her.

Henry and Elaine made their first formal visit to the Hartwicks on a Sunday afternoon in late September, maneuvering through a grid of hard-packed dirt roads miles from their university. Henry, enjoying a rare day away from the heaped books in his library carrel, sang out at the dark soil and rich green crops, Elaine laughing at his excitement. Their car pitched over unseen railroad tracks camouflaged by a growth of thick weeds. "We're in the fertility belt," he cried, reaching back to squeeze Joy's small foot.

Stuart and Winnie had rented a large white house overwhelmed by vines and sagging branches far from neighbors in a farming township called Oxford.

"I know it's rather isolated here," Stuart said to Henry in lieu of a greeting as they shook hands in the foyer, "but I've always wanted to live in Oxford."

His face suddenly reddened as deep chuckles rumbled from his middle. It was one of the few intentional jokes Henry ever heard Stuart make.

"And it's just right for Stuart to do his research," Winnie added. "He needs absolute quiet."

Every now and then she brightened with little outbursts of enthusiasm that Henry found attractive. Usually, she was a plain woman with pallid skin and drab hair.

Inside the living room of overstuffed chairs and family antiques he had shipped from back East, Stuart sat, crossed his legs, and sipped sherry. Winnie poured from a decanter for Henry and Elaine, then put Joy in the playpen with Tink.

"She's so dainty," Winnie said. Even though the babies were only a week apart in birth dates, Tink was a head taller and five pounds heavier. Joy, in pink tights and frilly white visiting dress, sucked on her pacifier while the boy hugged a stuffed panda and scowled.

The mothers took chairs near the playpen, and Henry found himself across the room with Stuart, glancing over at the babies, fascinated by his daughter's play. When Tink reached out a tentative hand and touched Joy's face, his blood surged. "Cute boy you have," he told Stuart, suddenly warming to the man.

Stuart fell into a coughing fit.

Henry looked away through a doorway into a room filled with precisely shelved books, many leather bound, totally unlike his own shaggy paperbacks stuffed into orange crates. He envied the man that room, a sanctuary where for several hours each day he could be alone with his own mind, where neither wife nor child could interrupt the pleasure of contemplation, the thrill of insights.

Stuart stood and led him inside, announcing that he had done the fine binding himself, precisely summarizing the technique. He reached to an upper shelf and slipped out several thin volumes in brown leather. "I'd like to show you my diaries."

Henry took the one offered and ran fingertips over the gold-leafed tooling, then opened into the unlined pages of immaculate italic lettering. The heading for each entry was written out in full: Friday, September the twenty-first, Nineteen hundred and eighty-three. Henry, fascinated, closed his eyes to breathe in the leather scent, pressed a palm against the fine rag paper. After turning a few pages, he realized the pattern of the entries: first the exact time of Stuart's rising, a sentence or two on the weather, a summary of the day's activities, usually something like "nine hours at my desk with Saint-Beuve," and finally summaries of his insights.

Now Henry became curious. He took another volume from Stuart's hand, one that ended only a month before, and flipped through in search of something truly personal, an emotion, a note of upset or caring, a reference to Winnie or Tink. But Coleridge dominated. Stuart had been watching him with close expectation. Henry returned the diaries into his hands and said, truthfully, that they were beautiful books.

II

When the Hartwicks made their return visit to the apartment Henry and Elaine rented in town, Elaine fussed for hours, dusting and redusting, straightening the prints, stacking stray books, repositioning chairs six inches this way or that.

"Would you like me to repaper the walls?" Henry asked.

"It's so tiny and cluttered here. This place wasn't meant for a baby."

"We'll sell Joy. Trade her in on a Chippendale end table."

"Winnie has such lovely things. China. A silver tea service."

"And Stuart is the most cultivated man I know." Henry paused to smile. "He's got cultivation coming out of his ears."

"Like stuffing. He's the stuffiest man I've ever met."

"But we've got charm, wit, and winning ways. An afternoon with us will make Stuart grovel with envy."

Just as he spoke the man's name, the door buzzer sounded, exactly at the arranged time. Winnie carried a squirming Tink and a shoulder bag of bottles and diapers. Stuart held only a tissue-wrapped gift Bordeaux and a marked volume in his other hand. "There's a passage I've been wanting to show you," he told Henry.

Elaine accepted the wine and Winnie looked about for a place to deposit Tink while she ran back to the car for his toys and blanket. She stood holding the baby at arm's length, Stuart deliberately avoiding her eyes, as if he had arrived alone. Embarrassed, but not sure for whom, Henry took Tink from her and at once sensed a presence quite different from Joy. The boy twisted in his arms; strands of fine hair tickled his chin.

"Be careful," Stuart said. "It might be wet."

Winnie came back in seconds, retrieving her son and exclaiming how cozy the apartment was.

Stuart announced that he had been considering Longinus recently and began presenting insights as if he had prepared his conversation like a formal lecture. Henry had trouble following the man's ideas, sensing that he had entered a complex chain of thought rather late along the way.

Tink hit Joy with a plastic locomotive, Joy began to cry, and Winnie—mortified—gave her son a light swat on his thick pad of diaper. Outraged, he howled even louder than Joy. Each woman quickly embraced her child.

"He's been so cranky today," Winnie said by way of apology.

Elaine nodded. "Joy gets that way too."

The babies shrieked red-faced, mouth wide, gasping for breath.

"It's hard to imagine so much noise coming from such tiny creatures," Henry said to bridge the awkwardness.

But Stuart, pinpricks of sweat on his forehead, ignored him and spoke directly to Winnie. "If you can't control that child, get it out of this room!"

Elaine looked quickly to Henry and then down at the rug. "Maybe we can go into the bedroom," she said to Winnie, half whispering. Winnie nodded, and at once they disappeared with the babies.

The moment the door closed, Stuart resumed the bass drone of his discourse. Henry couldn't listen to a word of it. He sat shocked by the realization that this man scorned his own child.

III

For weeks the couples did not see each other, though Winnie called Elaine for long conversations several times every few days. "She's so lonely out there. When Stuart isn't using the car, he's closed off in his library."

Henry dreaded running into Stuart at the university, but he never did, until one afternoon the large man, his bulk buttoned into a blue blazer, approached him on the library steps. "I've been meaning to discuss a matter with you."

At once Henry assumed Stuart would explain his behavior toward his son. Instead he wanted to share thoughts about Lawrence Sterne, some elaborate thesis about the interplay between the temporal and the phenomenal and the atemporal and the noumenal. Henry tried to follow the argument, uncertain whether he was in the presence of genius or a bizarre form of madness.

"But Stuart," he could not help saying after ten minutes of anxious listening, "*Tristram Shandy* is a very funny book."

Stuart frowned, squashing his mustache. "I suppose it is," he said as if this were a new idea that must be digested very slowly.

Then he looked at his watch. "I didn't realize the time. I must be off to *my* Oxford." He gave one of his rare throat-clearing laughs. "*My* little center of learning."

"Regards to Winnie," he called after the man's broad back. Stuart grunted.

"And Tink." Silence.

IV

The next week, just one day after the doctor confirmed Elaine's suspicion that she was pregnant again, Winnie called while Elaine had Joy at the park. Henry, coat on and eager to spend the afternoon in his carrel, explained that she would be back in an hour.

"I know she's not home," Winnie said. "She told me this morning. I have to talk with you."

"Yes?" Henry sensed great import in her tone. He paused, expecting her to go on.

"Not on the phone." He realized she was whispering. "Stuart is letting me have the car for shopping. Can we meet in town?"

Henry agreed, even though it meant rearranging his day, taking time from his research, without the slightest idea of what she might want.

When Henry arrived, Winnie was waiting in the Sears parking lot, Tink asleep in a bassinet on the back seat of the ponderous station wagon.

"Would you like a cup of coffee?" Henry asked, not sure what they would do with the baby.

"Can we just talk in the car?"

"Fine." He got in beside her and met her eyes, noticing for the first time how vulnerable they were. Her hands rubbed the steering wheel. "What did you want to talk about?'

Winnie breathed deeply and looked away from him, straight out the windshield. "Tink was an accident."

He waited for more, something of significance, but finally said, "So was Joy. We'd planned to wait."

"I mean a real accident." Tears ran down the side of her nose. "Stuart never wanted children."

She was sobbing and Henry realized what he should have known weeks before. "Have you told Elaine?" he asked.

"I've been too ashamed to tell anyone. Then I saw you holding Tink. You're such a wonderful father."

She lifted his hand and pressed the knuckles to her burning cheek. Embarrassed, he let her tears fall onto his flesh and waited through the long silence until she finally released him.

He squeezed her hand. "Tink is a sweet, handsome boy. Stuart will come to love him."

Her sobs discomforted him, almost made him guilty for loving his own wife and child so much.

Before she drove away, as Henry was starting his car, Winnie called out to him. "Please promise me that you'll never say anything about today to Elaine. She's my best friend."

At home he found Elaine and Joy napping on the big double bed and lay down to pull them into his embrace. He placed his open hand on Elaine's stomach even though he knew signs of life were months away.

V

The invitation came in the mail, a gold embossed card with date and time entered in Stuart's italic hand.

"I'll call and claim morning sickness." Elaine slipped it into a stack of journals.

"I thought you liked Winnie," Henry said.

"She's sweet and sad. But I won't spend another afternoon watching Stuart treat that poor child like a creature turned up on a slimy log."

"I'll play with him. Practice for a boy."

"Stuart will seal you off in that library the second you come through the door. That's my idea of hell."

"But imagine his library in this apartment. A room that's not cluttered with racks of drying diapers where I could do my work in peace. No more cage of a carrel. My books and my family. Only having to open a door to get from one to the other."

"Is that your Oxford?"

"I don't need a magic city. My life can be perfect anywhere." He kissed her and pulled the bulge of her middle tight against him.

"Do we have to visit Stuart and Winnie?"

He nodded, annoyed by the burden of Winnie's secret.

VI

At twilight, Henry drove away from their second visit to the Hartwicks in Oxford, lulled himself into a delicious dream of his family in a house like that, he with his walls of books, Elaine with her crafts studio, Joy and the new baby in their nursery.

Joy, missing her nap, slept on Elaine's lap, her face rubbing against her mother's breast as the car bounced along the deserted country road. Henry prolonged the silence, unwilling to open a conversation that would unleash Elaine's dislike of Stuart. Of course the day had been a disaster, Stuart practically ripping Tink from Henry's arms when he tried to hold the boy, Winnie sniffling back tears the whole time. He'd wanted to punch Stuart, drive his fist into the man's puffed face. No more. He made a private vow never to go back. He'd stay out of other people's lives. He had his own family to care about.

The rich glow of the horizon dazzled his eyes. He blinked and noticed the wooden X of the crossing sign, recalling the surprising thump of tracks from the first time they drove the route. Elaine brushed Joy's fine curls with her lips and hummed. The sign's paint was weathered down to bare wood, a poorly tended relic, Henry thought, of long past travelers.

At the sudden thunder of engine noise, his mind hung suspended in indecision, as if it were an enormous weight balanced just inside the windshield. Then he yanked the wheel and swerved, but the impact blew off the driver's door and threw him out of the car, away from the mangled steel that crushed his wife and daughter.

VII

Henry lay in a coma three weeks and spent four months in a body cast. Both legs suffered compound breaks; three ribs were cracked, his skull fractured, a lung punctured.

When he was out of traction, several weeks before his release, Winnie came to visit.

"Tink is with a sitter," she told him as if that explanation were vital.

"Yes."

"I wanted to see you right away, but they weren't allowing visitors. And then when you were conscious again my life fell apart."

"Oh."

"Stuart left us." She caught her breath. "One day he collected all his things, all his books and papers, packed the station wagon, and drove back East. I stood there and screamed the whole time. Tink was screaming too, but I couldn't even pick him up."

"I'm sorry."

She stopped talking and went pale. "Oh my god! I'm the one who should be sorry."

"I'd rather not talk about it," he said. She nodded, again and again.

"Tell me about you," he said to make her stop.

"It's just Tink and me now. We moved to an apartment in town. I couldn't stay in that house in Oxford. Stuart's mother sends money. There's plenty of money. I try to believe that Tink will be better off away from a father who despises him."

"You're probably right."

Winnie put her hand next to his on the crisp white sheet, and it struck him how alive it was, that it could touch and feel. That it was the wrong hand.

"What will you be doing now?" she asked. Her fingers trembled.

He buried his hand beneath the blanket. "Go away. I wish I could find a place a million miles from here."

VIII

Through the endless immobile days, unable to read, unwilling to watch television, Henry had envisioned Stuart's library, the walls of shelves, the odor of hand-tooled bindings, the deep impression of print on creamy pages. He imagined the books so often they became transformed into his own possessions, a room he had never known before, four walls filled from floor to ceiling with thousands of leather volumes. No door, no window, just a thick wool rug and a carved wooden chair. A place where he could shut out all other thoughts.

But the day the doctor, always gravely polite, told him that he would be released, he let himself remember the apartment he had lived in with Elaine and Joy—the shabby graduate student furniture, the prints cut from art magazines, but most of all the paperbacks wedged into wooden crates. He would have torn those books apart, burned them in one great bonfire, sworn a pledge never to read again if that would have returned his wife and child.

When he moved, he abandoned all possessions, but a thousand miles away he accumulated new books and read for hours each day. He justified his life through research, as if each note he took were a small payment exacted by some terrible debt. At night, when he could not sleep, he lifted a volume from his night table and snapped on the reading light.

IX

Over the years, Henry slowly admitted the world into his life, first accepting invitations for dinner, then for weekend gatherings, finally traveling to new places, cataloguing views and vistas in his notes.

He lost his dread of women, eventually lived with one, then another, and for three years a nurse called Barbara. But she took a job a thousand miles away, weeping for the first time the morning of her leaving. "You're a kind, sweet man. But you never let me know you."

"If I ever loved anyone so much again," Henry told her, "I'd spend every moment of every day in terror."

X

Years later, on a leave in Oxford, Henry converted dollars to pounds at the Barclay's Bank branch on the High Street and walked toward Carfax. He noticed a large man in British tweeds and a six-foot scarf staring at him from the grey wall of Queen's College.

"I say," the man called to him. "Don't I know you?"

The bass voice made Henry look closer. Immediately, he felt a desperate sinking. It was Stuart Hartwick, thirty pounds heavier, the patch of mustache all grey now.

"It's Henry of course." Stuart gave a ceremonial wave. "I always assumed we would meet again."

Henry resisted the impulse to run. Instead he said, "I see you've finally gotten to the real Oxford."

"Quite." Stuart seemed to miss the allusion to his old joke. "I've followed your career with interest, Henry. Read your books and articles. They're not my way of seeing things of course. But apparently you've made a success for yourself."

"I'm afraid I don't keep up as much as I should. I've missed your work."

"I don't find it necessary to publish." Stuart cleared his throat. "Well, Henry, what brings you here?"

"A grant. And you?"

"Newman and the Oxford Movement, of course."

"Where are you teaching?"

"I don't teach." Stuart seemed offended. "I've never taught."

Henry took a long look at his watch, savoring each tick as if it held an eternity. "I'd better eat something before my appointment." He stepped away.

"Excellent. I'll join you."

Henry, ashamed at his helplessness, led Stuart to a pub in a 14th century courtyard off Cornmarket away from the midday bustle where he normally enjoyed the steak and kidney, the lukewarm bitter in quiet solitude. They sat at one corner of a crowded table, Henry on a stool, Stuart on the wall bench beside a tiny old lady with rouged cheeks and shopping bundles piled on her lap.

"It's rather awkward for me at this moment," Stuart said

"In what way?"

"Stuart is here. In Oxford."

After a second Henry realized he meant his son, Tink.

"At which college?"

Stuart snorted.

"None. He came here two days ago to track me down."

"How is he?"

"I have no idea. I haven't seen him in years."

"But you said he's here."

"I've managed to avoid him so far. But he left a note at my bank."

"The bank?"

Once again, Henry felt bewildered by one of Stuart's explanations.

"My address is a secret. I hope he won't recognize me on the street."

"Your son?"

"I've chosen to have no part of paternity."

The old lady set her mouth and clutched her packages. "But what does Winnie think of all this?"

"That," Stuart said as if suppressing great anger, "is another story."

He did not explain, silently slicing his gammon steak while Henry, with a sudden pang, recalled the long-forgotten warmth of babies in his arms.

XI

A pounding on the apartment door awoke Henry at 6 a.m. It was still dark outside. He sat up in bed and called, "What is it?" The pounding sounded louder. He rubbed his eyes, ran fingers through his hair, and realized he had to use the toilet. "Just a minute," he called. When he came back, he put on slippers and a pair of trousers.

A pudgy young man stood on his doorstep, dressed in rumpled blue denim, a rucksack strapped over his shoulders. A wispy beard grew on a red-rashed chin. Henry knew the soft brown eyes at once.

"Where's my father?" the boy demanded.

"I have no idea. How did you get this address?"

"He left it at his bank. In case of emergency. I spent the night finding the damn street. It's all crooked alleys in this town."

Henry's neck tensed, but he only sighed resignation. Still half asleep, he held the door wide. "Come inside, Tink."

The young man froze. "Where did you get that name?"

"I knew you when you were a baby." Henry gestured toward an armchair.

Tink let the rucksack slide off his shoulder and collapsed into the cushions. Only then did Henry recognize his exhaustion. He offered coffee, but Tink shook his head.

"How is your mother?" Henry saw a hand trembling on a white sheet.

"The same as always."

"What's does she do?"

"Nothing." Tink frowned. "Nobody is our family does anything. We all live off Grandma's money. My mother spends her days polishing the silver. She can count butter knives for hours."

"Why are you so angry with her?"

"She just gave up when my father walked out."

Henry's hand tingled with the sensation of her burning cheek, the touch of her tears on his knuckles. "She loved you so much."

Tink glared. "She treats me like a victim. Her poor abandoned baby."

He slouched in the chair, mouth drooping bleakly. Yet Henry studied him with rapt concentration, suddenly realizing that Tink was a long-awaited visitor. He spoke very slowly. "You used to play with my daughter."

Tink gave him a blank look.

"Her name was Joy," Henry said, wondering if Tink could sense the pain it cost him to speak it aloud after so many years.

XII

Tink dozed and Henry watched him, imagining what it would be like to search for Stuart in Oxford. He would try all the obvious places—the Bodleian, Blackwell's, up and down Broad Street and narrow Turl, the Ashmolean Museum, and finally some of the college chapels—Merton, Christ Church, Pembroke. Then it occurred to him that Newman's college had been Oriel. But he knew Stuart would no longer be in that library, the porter explaining how Mr. Hartwick had suddenly packed all his papers and rushed off.

Henry pictured catching Stuart at the train station, grabbing him by the lapels and shouting, "Your son is in my flat." And Stuart brushing away his hands. "That woman violated our agreement. No children. My work requires absolute freedom from the ordinary."

With a toe, Henry touched the bulging rucksack on his rug, pushed against the dead weight.

XIII

"What will you do now?" Henry asked Tink after he awoke, as they drank instant coffee and ate crackers.

"Go home. Look for a room. Find a job. I won't sponge off Grandma the rest of my life the way my father does."

"Why did you come here, Tink?"

Tink looked down at his shoes. "To make him admit he has a son."

"He doesn't know how to be a father, Tink."

"Most men do it every day."

"Yes. It's the most natural thing in the world."

Tink stood and gripped a canvas strap, ready to leave.

Henry stood with him and held his arm. "Did your mother ever tell you about me?" he asked urgently.

"About what?"

Henry scanned the room, overwhelmed by foreignness, the buckled wallpaper, the ancient fixtures, the scarred bookcases. He gripped the back of a loveseat. "The accident."

Tink shook his head, then blinked with surprise. "Were you the ones?"

"My family." Henry dug fingers into the upholstery as if a great force was about to blast him though the sealed walls that had been his safety.

"Whenever she tells that story, she ends up crying."

"I've never let myself cry." Henry clutched even tighter, pressed his feet down into the rug.

"She made my father invite you."

"I accepted it."

"To be with them? Why?"

For you. But Henry did not speak aloud, amazed at the memory of his motive, at the strangeness of having this grown man standing before him, at all the years separating him from his own life. "I'm glad you came," Henry finally said.

Tink hoisted the rucksack onto his shoulders.

Henry saw himself taking Winnie's hand in the hospital. The idea had seemed preposterous then, awful in a grief so absolute it numbed his soul. If not Winnie, some other woman, some other child. "It didn't have to be this way," he said, looking back at a stranger's bookcases.

"What?"

"Forget about him, about her. Choose your own life."

He watched closely as Tink descended the stairs, each worn step thumping under his weight. When the front door closed, he crossed to the window and saw Tink in the street, pausing briefly and then swept off in the morning flow of the waking city—clerks with thick briefcases, old women on bicycles, undergraduates trailing long striped scarves, school-children skipping beside stone walls.

A glowing sunrise dazzled the soaring spires. Tink stepped with the others toward the bright rays and then turned a corner. Henry imagined him walking all day, never looking back, suddenly discovering something new that would change his life.

He swung the windows wide and felt the breeze on his face, heard human voices rise from the street around him, the laughter of the children. With an ache of longing, he reached his arms toward all the life of Oxford.

BAGGAGE

HOWARD CAUGHT A LOCAL FROM PARIS TO LILLE to board the Lombardy Express to Rome there at five in the afternoon. With all his rushing to make connections he had not eaten anything all day but a breakfast croissant. Now he was hungry and annoyed with himself for bringing too much luggage for the trip: an overpacked black pullman case strapped onto a chrome pull cart, a matching one-suiter, and a carry-on shoulder bag weighted down with a camera, tape recorder, transistor radio, and voltage converter. All that paraphernalia for one solitary traveler. What a fool he was.

But he had expected to find a city where he could linger, slowly unpack his possessions into spacious drawers, stroll peacefully through empty streets, seek pictures that satisfied, record sounds that pleased. But each city disappointed. Crowds pushed him along sidewalks past hostile stares from the cafes. Every time he stopped to aim his camera, a blur of arm or head ruined the scene in the viewfinder. The oppression of strangers: bodies bumping against him, a din of harsh foreignness in his ears, a thousand shrugs in his face. Nowhere was there a smile for him alone.

Under his load Howard stumbled down the corridor with the lurching of the train, squeezing past the people standing at the windows until he located the compartment with his seat number. His stomach tightened when he saw the young man settled between the armrests. He produced his reservation card, held it out in front of him. But as he was about to speak, the young man met his gaze with soft brown eyes, and Howard could feel the stares of the others just beyond the edge of his vision. He sensed that they liked the young man, were ready to side with him against Howard's protest. But he would not give them the satisfaction. He just held his card and waited, refusing to look at anyone. The young man finally stood with muttered apologies, grabbed a small canvas bag, and hurried out the sliding door.

Howard found the compartment too crowded to disconnect the pullman case from its cart and fold the frame. So he hoisted it up over his head to the one empty spot on the luggage rack and forced his one-suiter atop it. The carry-on bag he kept on the floor under his seat.

He squirmed for comfort, felt a flush prickle his face, pretended to lose himself in the intricacies of resetting his watch because the others in the compartment were all studying him. Slowly, secretly, he looked back at them.

He sat in the middle across from a heavy old woman whose dress rode above her knees to expose rolled stocking tops. Closest to the door were two young girls, perhaps nineteen or twenty, one blonde and pink-cheeked with perfect white teeth, the other with piercing green eyes and thick auburn hair twisted into a severe knot. She was not as pretty as her friend. Both were as young as the daughters he had not seen in more than a year.

The other two people in the compartment, a man and a woman, took his attention. Sitting across from each other by the window, they looked so unlike. She was fair, plump, and freckled, her dress too tight, ovals of pale flesh showing where the buttonholes stretched across her middle. The man had a flowing black mustache and goatee that matched rich, wavy hair. He was dark and handsome, tightly muscled in expensive jeans and a black turtleneck. Howard watched for a time and saw that they did not acknowledge each other. She must have been alone.

But just as he considered smiling at her, the woman leaned forward, touched the man's knee, and whispered. The man responded with a burst of musical Italian, all eye rollings and hand gestures. She kissed her finger and reached it to his lips.

Howard turned away to the landscape rushing past the window. His clenched fists trembled with anger. He would not speak, he would not utter a sound during the entire trip to Rome. No matter what they said to him, no matter how they said it, he would feign ignorance of all languages and stay absolutely apart.

By the time the train reached Valenciennes, Howard was no longer a disruption to the compartment, just one more object in the clutter, familiar enough to be ignored in such close quarters. He felt relief that no one addressed him while he planned his incomprehension.

The old woman reached into her sack of a handbag to pull out a sandwich wrapped in white paper and a small bottle of red wine sealed with foil. She unfolded the paper in her lap and took a deep bite into the bread, tearing at meat and crust. Crumbs dropped onto the front of her dress and a spicy salami odor filled the compartment. The others did not pay attention to her, but Howard's stomach felt hollow with hunger and a weakness spread through his limbs. He tried to close his eyes.

When he opened them, he found the green-eyed girl looking right at him. Flustered, he made a gesture of cutting with a knife, brought an imaginary fork to his mouth, and pointed questioningly out at the corridor. He guessed the French for dining car would be wagon a manger or voiture a manger. But he tried neither, still resolved not to speak.

The girl glanced at her friend and shook her head. "Non," she said, "non." The others began to attempt explanations, the old woman with words that occasionally sounded French but had a guttural German pronunciation, the man in rapid Italian, finally the woman with him in crystal-clear British English: "I'm afraid there is no dining car on this train. There will be vendors at some of the stations in France. But other than those, you'll have to wait until we get to Italy in the morning and a food cart comes on board." Howard kept the understanding out of his eyes and screwed up his face at her.

"Perhaps he's Spanish," the pretty girl said in English to the woman, the z-like s's the only hint of her accent.

"He is not handsome enough," her friend said in a French simple enough for Howard to decipher.

The pretty girl giggled. "Le Scandinave?" The green-eyed girl shrugged indifference.

The English woman said something in Italian to the man, touching his knees again. It was obvious that she liked to touch him. The old woman just chewed on her sandwich.

The pretty girl began a conversation with the English woman. "Do you speak French as well as you speak Italian?"

"I'm afraid not. I studied Italian at university. My French is rather poor."

"I have been learning English since I was ten."

"You're quite good."

The girl nodded thanks. "How long will you be visiting Italy?"

"We're going home. We live there. Outside Bologna. In Budrio."

"You and your husband?"

"He's not my husband." The man beamed a smile at the girl as she blushed. Her friend smirked.

Howard wanted to laugh, but he sat blankly, darting his eyes from face to face of the others in a show of confusion. Then he settled on the English woman, trying to decide if she were attractive.

She couldn't have been past her late twenties but dressed dowdily, with a grey sweater buttoned around her shoulder and square-toed shoes. She was overweight, but her look was pleasant, the mouth a bit too wide, the lipstick too thick and too orange, the hair unflattering, not long enough for her round face.

She had several magazines wedged between her side and the compartment wall. Howard would like to have read them to fill the time but could not ask without exposing his English.

He stood, slung his carry-on bag over his shoulder, and stepped over the girls' feet to slide the door back and move out into the corridor. At the end of the car the young man who had been in his seat sat on the flap that folded out from the wall. He nodded as Howard passed him to enter the toilet, and it struck Howard that he must be a friend of the two girls, perhaps the lover of one, of the green-eyed girl.

A sign in four languages warned that the water was not suitable for drinking. Howard splashed it on his face but would not look in the mirror. Then he stepped on the flush pedal and watched the ground flash by under the hole until someone tapped on the door.

He opened it for the Italian and was surprised by how short the man was. Sitting he had looked tall. "Scusi," the man said. "Grazia."

When the Italian returned to the compartment and sat beside Howard, the English woman produced their food, fruit and cheese. Again Howard suffered hunger pangs and wanted them to offer him something, so badly he might have responded to English. But he could see that they had barely enough for themselves.

Later, when the train was pulling in to Metz, the Italian nudged him and pointed to the vendor's cart on the platform. Howard ran to the door of the car while the train eased to a stop with a creak of brakes. By the time they came to rest the cart was far back. He jumped down and hurried to stand in line; but, just as his turn came, the train began to move. The vendor shouted, a conductor called. Howard grabbed a bottle of beer and shoved a twenty franc note into the vendor's hand. Clutching the beer, feeling like a fool, he leaped back on the train without his change. He had to walk through seven cars to get back to his compartment. The Italian gave him an opener for the beer. Although she did not make a sound, he was sure the green-eyed girl was laughing at him.

The old woman was digging through her handbag again, groping until she pulled out a ragged packet of rubber-banded papers. A brown passport slipped out with it and fluttered to the floor behind her shoe, unseen. She unfolded several sheets, read them closely, and returned the packet, finally realizing her passport was gone. She clasped hands beneath her chin and let out an exclamation of woe. The two girls, immediately solicitous, turned to her and listened to her fragmented explanation, the green-eyed one trying to keep her on track with questions.

They had her empty the handbag item by item, spreading across the seat an assortment of plastic cases, combs, medicine vials, a balled cloth that might have been a nightgown. The couple moved to help also, the man poking a hand behind the seat cushion, the woman scanning the floor. The old woman still obscured the passport with her shoe.

Howard knew all he had to do was point, reach out an arm, extend a finger. But he did not want to call attention to himself; he did not want to become one of them. Then the pretty girl bent down on her knees and saw behind the woman's foot. She held the passport in the air like a trophy. The old woman made a gesture as if to embrace her. The others grinned and the girl blushed happily.

By the time they left the stop in Strasbourg, it was dark outside, the six passengers reflected in the compartment window. Howard took the tape recorder from his carry-on bag and, through the earplug, listened to a tape he had made from his radio in Paris: static, the blur of tuning, music, a babble of voices in French, German, Spanish, Dutch, Italian, all cut off in midsentence as he had switched from station to station in search of something he could understand.

When the conductor came in to convert the compartment to couchette bunks, they had to step out into the corridor and take down their luggage from the racks. The Italian did most of the shifting, passing out the suitcases, the girls' nylon bags, and the old woman's cord-tied cardboard box to Howard and the conductor.

The conductor folded up the luggage racks, pulled a ladder from under the left seat, folded out the seatbacks to make the middle bunks, and swung down the top bunks from the wall. Howard would be in the middle. Before the conductor passed out sheet, pillows, and blankets, the

Italian rearranged the luggage, stacked most of it in the space over the door on the ceiling of the corridor. The old woman's box and Howard's pullman had to stand in the middle of the floor. Howard brought has carry-on into his bunk.

The old woman would sleep across from him, the girls in the lower bunks, the English woman and the Italian man on top. Howard kept bumping into the old woman as they spread their sheets and blankets. The green- eyed girl looked up at him while he fumbled to make his bed. When the English woman climbed the ladder and swung her legs onto the bunk, Howard could see her white thighs above the tops of her stockings. She reached out to clasp the Italian's hand, and Howard was furious at his aloneness.

He could not sleep. The old woman fluted high-pitched snoring. His stomach twisted with hunger spasms. The train wheels slapped endlessly at the metal rails. He tossed and squirmed, shut in, claustrophobic. Because the curtains in the compartment were pulled to block all light, he could not see his watch and kept sliding the door open an inch or two to check the time.

At five-thirty, with the first glow of dawn, he contorted into his shoes and got up to use the toilet. Then he stood at the window in the corridor to look out at the Italian-Swiss Alps. Snow peaks and shadowed crags, a few cars far below on the highway, the lights of distant houses, and every now and then a village, unmoving and immaculately clean. The cleanliness of Switzerland made him feel scummy. His head itched; he had not brushed his teeth. He tugged down the window to let cold air blast his face.

Later, when the others were all up, the old woman and the girls standing in line for the toilet, the Italian restored the compartment from couchettes to riding seats. He replaced the luggage on the racks, stood on his toes to slide the old woman's box over the door. Only Howard's pullman would not fit easily into the new arrangement. The Italian left it on the floor and shrugged at him. But when the girls and the woman returned, there was not enough room for everyone's feet.

Howard pretended not to notice. But the green-eyed girl kicked his foot. He glared at her and quickly shoved his case onto the rack above the old woman while she looked up apprehensively. He wished she were not on the train, with her rolled stockings and her salami and her passport and her cardboard box. If she were gone, there would be enough room for the rest of them; he would not feel so crushed in with strangers.

They were in Italy now, stopping for a long time in Chaisso where Howard tripped against the green-eyed girl in his rush to get at the food cart being pushed down the corridor. He overpaid for a banana, a cup of lukewarm coffee, and a piece of stale raisin cake that still did not satisfy his hunger.

When the train passed Como and moved onto the open countryside of Lombardy, the French girls began to read paperbacks and the English woman and Italian man made eyes at each other, knowing—Howard was sure—that they were only a few hours from a bed.

The trip seemed bumpier now, Howard pitching from side to side in his seat, feeling vibrations through his shoes. He looked up to see his pullman case sliding loose from the rack above the old woman, rattling inch by inch across the dark crossbars, the wheels of the pull cart scraping against the ceiling. Two more inches and it would fall.

He knew he should shout to her to look out. But the sound lodged in his throat like an enormous mass. He tried to lift his hands, but they lay paralyzed in his lap.

The Italian saw and lunged forward with a cry. But he was too late. The case tumbled down, bounced off the old woman's knees, and struck her across the ankles with the chrome bar of the frame.

She let out a long wail of pain. The pretty girl burst into tears; her green-eyed friend pushed Howard's case off the woman, opening the doors and forcing it out into the corridor as if it were a vicious animal. The English woman embraced the old woman, the Italian kneeling at her feet. Howard rubbed a hand at his throat, clutching against the sensation that he would choke on swallowed words.

The old woman's stockings were shredded, blood streaming from a deep ugly gash in her right instep. She moaned and wept and muttered a lament of pain. Both ankles swelled immediately, great purple bruises appearing through the holes in her stockings. The Italian unfolded a hand-kerchief and tied it around the gash.

The green-eyed girl disappeared into the corridor and came back with the young man who had been in Howard's seat. "L'etudiant en medicine," she announced. He pulled a first aid kit from his canvas bag, removed the handkerchief, cut away the stocking, cleaned the wound, and bandaged it. His work was quick and neat. He spoke soothingly to the old woman, who nodded and attempted to swallow her pain.

When the conductor finally came, the young man made a lengthy explanation, pointing to Howard, the rack, the pullman case in the corridor, while the conductor filled out a form.

"What will happen?" the English woman asked the green-eyed girl.

"We'll get off at Milan with her. The conductor is sending a radio message for an ambulance."

"Is her leg broken?"

"Jean doesn't think so. But it must be X-rayed."

At the central station in Milan the medical student and the Italian carried the woman off the train. The pretty girl took her suitcase and the green-eyed girl the cardboard box.

When they were all gone, Howard retrieved his pullman case from the corridor and placed it on the empty seat beside the English woman. He expected blood on the frame, but there was none. The four black wheels of the cart bounced on the cushion.

He thought of all his possessions inside, pictured them one by one in his head as he watched the bouncing. When he glanced up, he saw the English woman holding the handle with the identification tag that noted his American name and address.

She met his eyes and, barely moving her lips, spoke so softly Howard could not hear her curse.

THE HAPPY FRENCHMEN

WHEN DAN AND MARCY GOT OFF THE TRAIN IN LUGANO, they stepped from air conditioning into a wall of stagnant humidity. Sweat soaked their clothing by the time they reached the station steps and looked up at the grey sky suffocating the city. Dan squirmed in the stiff back brace, unfastened two more shirt buttons, swallowed his pain, and sucked in air, openmouthed.

Marcy looked miserable too, dragging the wheeled luggage across the platform. Her damp hair was matted to her forehead, flat against her temples. Because his dislocated sacroiliac made him helpless, she had to be the one to hoist their bags up and down from luggage racks while he blushed embarrassment, hoping the world would sense his debility.

"This is hell," she said.

"I picked Lugano because it's supposed to be so beautiful." He tried to imagine the city without the grey haze—the palm trees under brilliant sun, lush gardens, mountains out to the horizon, a glimmering lake in the harbor below.

Marcy's eyes were red, her round face drained of color. Yet, as miserable as she looked, Dan felt himself drawn to the curve of her tight white slacks. He desired her there in that heat, pain stabbing across his hip and down his left leg. He couldn't stop desiring her. She gave him a sad smile, and his heart plunged like a stone.

•

For the week before he flew to Zurich as part of the company team for a trade show, Dan had tossed sleepless with expectation, Beatrice's weight on the mattress beside him, their children in rooms across the hallway, his nights filled with imagining Marcy. On the plane, alone, Marcy gone ahead for final preparations, her presence was so real he felt that he had only to reach out and embrace her. She was his palpable future. With his long hours and frequent travel, he only saw the kids on weekends anyway.

And what kind of a life was it for Beatrice—married to a man obsessed with someone else?

In Europe, for the first time in all the months they had been lovers, they would finally spend the night together. At home, he had a wife waiting. On their domestic trips together, Marcy treated him as no more than a co-work-er, fearful of her reputation in the company. Dan couldn't bring himself to tell her what the men in the cafeteria said as they sat by the windows watching her run the paths outside in jogging shorts, joking that the speed of her promotions came in direct proportion to the length of her legs. Even before he had loved her, she figured in his fantasies—a lithe divorcee with a beachfront condo and a red Jaguar. Afterward, he had to swallow his fury at the others' innuendo, caging the impulse to lash out in outraged pride.

They had spent whole evenings planning their European tryst, Mar-cy insisting on reviewing every detail of the strategy. They would arrive separately for the trade show, book into different hotels, speak only of business, never share meals unless part of a group, spread stories that he would extend this trip for a weekend in Paris, she for summer skiing on Jungfrau. Dan chose their true private destination, recalling Lugano as the honeymoon site of a couple he had met once on a plane.

Dan opened the city map he had been studying throughout the train ride as a futile diversion from the torture of his back. "The hotel's only a block away."

She pointed at the rooftops directly beneath them. "Straight down."

The train station sat on a steep hill overlooking the city. To the right Dan could see the dome of the cathedral, to the left the sign for their hotel. Twisting steps chiseled into the rockface led down to the street below. It was a sheer drop from here to there.

Marcy stood beside their luggage at the curbside, her feet in narrow sandals bound with thin white straps, the toenails gleaming red. Dan looked at the shape of her feet and wanted to weep. Swallowing, he sig-naled for a taxi.

Marcy counted the suitcases as the driver loaded them in the trunk. They could abandon everything for all Dan cared.

The taxi ride to the hotel was a series of tight downhill curves that kept lurching their bodies together in a contact that sent a twist of agony down his left leg. He closed his hand on her thigh to brace himself. She covered it with a light touch of fingertips, cool despite the heat of the day.

"How long has the weather been like this?" Dan asked the driver.

"All month, signore. Most always this is the most beautiful time of the ear."

"When will it break?"

The driver shrugged. "Who knows, signore. Let's hope you and your signora bring good fortune."

•

That morning, back in Zurich after the trade show ended and all the others had boarded limousines for the airport, Dan rushed to Marcy's hotel the second she called. In her room, he twisted the bolt and fixed the chain, murmuring his love the whole time, tear-blinded with joy at the press of her body, her arching gasp of pleasure.

Afterwards he put a hand on her chest to feel her pulse subside. When she was calm, he leaned over her and touched his lips to her forehead. She closed her eyes. "I just want to go on like this."

For the rest of our lives."

"I mean taking one day at a time."

Dan stared down at her, elbows locked, arms rigid, as if his limbs had turned to stone. "I want to marry you." He had meant to give the words the force of his conviction, but they came out as a plea.

She still would not look at him. Tears eased out from under her eyelids. He watched them spread down her cheeks. "So much could happen," she said. "It's such a huge risk."

"I'll take it. Nothing else matters."

"I don't want you to ruin your marriage for me."

"It's ruined without you."

"You don't know," she cried. "You're not seeing clearly. Everything is so complicated."

She shook with sobs and Dan began to kiss her tears, at first slowly, tasting salt, then harder and faster, Marcy clinging back until they were making love again. But when it was over, before he could speak, she said, "Nothing's changed."

"What about Lugano?"

"We'll be wonderful in Lugano, and then we'll go home."

•

The bellhop, a small, furtive man with a thick black mustache, couldn't undo the straps on their luggage carts, turning them sideways and up-side-down in an effort to free the suitcases. "Never mind!" Marcy cried. The man dropped a cart with a thud that snapped the straps loose. Dan gave him a double tip and pushed him out the door.

"Look at this room." Marcy threw up her hands.

With the luggage on the floor, there was barely space to maneuver around the bed. The dark floral wallpaper clashed with the heavy striped drapes. The carpeting was worn, the faded brown bedspread dotted with cigarette burns.

"And it's not even airconditioned," she added. "I'll open a window."

She seized his arm. "Don't you move. You'll do something else terrible to your back. I can't stand to see you suffering this way."

"I try not to talk about my pain."

"Your face gives you away. It's nothing but one constant grimace."

For the first time, it struck Dan that she might be annoyed with him.

•

At midday in Zurich, after he left Marcy's room to pick up his luggage at his own hotel, stomach fluttering as if a terrified bird were trapped inside, Dan had dislocated his sacroiliac stepping into the elevator. As he shifted weight to his left leg, something tore in his side, a sensation that his innards had ripped loose, so painful he had to grip a handle for support and then stand hyperventilating for five minutes before he dared try to reach his room, hugging the walls and dragging his leg all the way.

Once inside he immediately applied icepacks, unwilling to call Marcy and tell her what had happened. I'll be all right for the trip, he kept reassuring himself, although he knew weeks of agony lay ahead.

An hour before train time, he had stared at the ceiling with burning, sleepless eyes, wondering how he would be able to engineer himself up from the mattress. Despite his resolution to grit his teeth and stand on the carpet with one thrust, he could barely lift his shoulders from the pillow, and had to slide his legs across the sheet and down along the side of the mattress, then grip the headboard and hoist himself into a sitting position. The maneuver left him whimpering. He counted to ten, but his nerve failed, then counted again and threw his feet to the floor, amazed at the courage it took to reach a vertical position. Standing, he hobbled to the closet, retrieved the brace he hadn't had to wear in two years, but packed at Beatrice's insistence, a wide canvas belt with a Velcro fastening and a hard plastic insert that wedged against the middle of his spine. When he strapped it on, he was able to take short, slow steps without the sensation of molten steel at his nerve endings.

•

"I need a nap," Marcy announced. "This heat is exhausting."

She kicked her slacks into a heap at the foot of the bed, then yanked her top over her head and stretched out in bikini underwear, forearm shielding her eyes.

Fatigued himself, the painkillers she carried in a little golden case numbing only his brain, he lay flat beside her, fully clothed, still in shoes and brace to avoid the burden of dressing later. Marcy rolled onto her side, facing the wall. He didn't think he would sleep but two hours later awoke disoriented at the roar of her blow dryer. She stood at the wall mirror angry with her hair for frizzing in the humidity.

"We'd better think about dinner," she told him.

Dan groaned inwardly. Now he would have to get up, and he was ashamed to ask for her help.

Clutching the edge of the mattress, he slid off onto the carpet, raised himself to his knees, and groped out toward the dresser for leverage.

"For God's sake, here!" Marcy gripped his elbows and pulled him upright. The aftershock that spasmed through his back muscles made him bite down on the insides of his cheeks. He didn't let himself cry out, but it took several minutes before he could catch his breath.

"Thank you," he said. "I'm sorry to be such a bother."

"I'm sorry you're suffering so much," she said, but he saw she was gritting her teeth.

•

When they got back to their room, Dan realized he had finished almost the entire bottle of dinner wine himself, while Marcy picked at the label with a fingernail. He sprawled back on the bed and couldn't keep his eyes from drooping shut. When Marcy pulled off his shoes, he tried to speak, but the words came out as a moan.

The next thing he knew sunlight was dazzling him and his head throbbed behind his sinuses. Marcy had thrown open the drapes. Behind the bathroom door the shower was hissing, then stopped with a wrenching in the pipes. She stepped back into the room drying herself, naked, water drops beaded on her flesh, breasts bobbling as she rubbed the towel across her back.

"You'd better get ready," she said. "We can't spend the day trapped in this place."

"Please, help me up."

She dropped the towel and reached her arms toward him. He gripped her shoulders while she lifted with a grunt, then sank against her until the back spasms subsided. She supported his weight inertly. He could feel her nipples against his chest. All he had to do was tilt her face up and kiss her. And then what? He was terrified at the thought of a sudden twisting.

This is crazy, he kept thinking with each deep breath. For months his desire had conjured moments like this. And now her embrace was only first aid.

In the shower he couldn't bend, just soaping his arms and chest and letting the water float the suds down his legs. Marcy was already dressed when he got out.

"It wasn't worth it," she said. "What wasn't."

"Bathing. Nine   in the   morning,   and I'm already soaked with perspiration. It's like living inside a sponge."

"Listen," he   offered, "we could check out now and head north somewhere. Up into the mountains."

"It's only a few days," she said. "We'll stick it out."

•

Dan wanted to try walking down the twisting narrow streets that led from their hotel to the center of the city, but Marcy insisted on a cab. "You don't have to prove anything," she told him.

The cab took them down to the central piazza, a large cobblestoned square of shops and umbrellaed cafe tables. Dan paid the driver, then thought to ask, "What's the best way to stay cool?"

"The lake, signore. You and the signora will find pleasant breezes on one of the steamers."

Marcy wanted to look in the jewelry store windows first, at the glimmering rows of rings and bracelets and earrings. As they approached the glass, Dan saw his reflection, a man moving with slow crabbed steps, hunched over and listing to one side. When she sought his opinion of a gold chain, he offered to buy her something.

She stiffened at the suggestion. "That's not why I asked."

"I just wanted you to have a souvenir."

"I'll remember this city without one."

The quay for the lake steamers was only a short walk from the square, across a wide boulevard thick with speeding cars. From the lakefront Dan could look back at the tiered levels of the city behind the spray of a large fountain. The peak of Mount Brè was barely visible in the haze, little more than an outline, like the shore across the lake.

Although the steamer wasn't scheduled to leave for another twenty minutes, Marcy wanted to board. "There's no point in waiting out on the street." He agreed. The cabin was stifling, so they took a bench on the stern, the first passengers of the trip.

Dan shielded his eyes from the glare and stared over the side, watching the water slap against the hull. It struck him that he would have to tell Beatrice something, how he had injured himself, why he hadn't flown right home. His real life seemed so vague now, here in this strange city, sitting beside the woman he had dreamed of loving. Dan didn't look around him until the boat began to back away from the pier and he discovered the deck crowded with people.

"Where'd everyone come from?" he asked Marcy.

"You weren't paying attention."

"They all want to escape the heat."

She nodded. "I've never spent a more unbearable day."

Despite the discomfort of the slat bench, Dan knew he had no choice but to sit. When the waitress came by, he ordered a beer. Marcy wanted nothing. Away from the shore, though the sun was strong, a light breeze blew over the deck.

He watched two children play at the railing, a brother and sister, both blond. The girl, about six or seven, was very pretty. Someday, he thought, she would be beautiful and wondered if her beauty would make her happy. The boy, a few years younger, hoisted himself up and hung over the railing, making sounds at the birds. His mother spoke sharply in German and pulled him down.

Dan listened for the languages around them. The boat was a babel—Swissdeutch, the Italian of the crew, Japanese, British English. But the French was loudest of all. He looked behind and saw three women with faces tilted up toward the sun's rays, one plump and middle-aged in what seemed to be a housedress, one young and plain in shorts, another young and quite lovely in jeans, her smile very appealing.

These women spoke softly. It was the four men across the aisle who blared their French, shouting conversation even though they were only a few feet apart. They swigged beer from bottles, in unison—glass to their lips, swallows, and arms down. Then they would look at each other and burst out laughing.

"They're drunk," Dan said to Marcy.

"They're just having a holiday."

"Why are they so lucky?"

She said nothing.

Like the women behind them, the men seemed mismatched—the loudest, with thick white hair and beard, was sunburned and bare-chested, a pale belly hanging over his belt; the old shrunken man on his right lit cigarette after cigarette with trembling hands. The two at either end were both much younger but total opposites—one impeccable with slick parted hair, horn-rimmed glasses, and a crisply pressed shirt, the other disheveled in an undershirt and cutoff trousers.

The bare-chested man unfolded his newspaper and passed out sheets to the three others, then gave step by step instructions on folding the paper into peaked caps. Even the old man made one, though he was slow and had to refold several times. But the bare-chested man was very patient. When all the hats were ready, he signaled that they should put them on their heads. He stood before them and saluted. They saluted back, again and again. Dan noticed that Marcy was watching closely, amused.

The bare-chested man plucked the hats from the others and stacked them atop his own. Then he crossed the deck to the three women, bowed, and adjusted a paper hat atop each of their heads. For a moment, Dan expected anger: the man was attempting a foolish pickup and would be abused. But the man leaned over and kissed the two younger women on both cheeks, the middle-aged on the mouth. It's his wife, Dan realized; they knew each other.

The women tipped hats to the other three men, and the men toasted them with beer bottles. Dan tried to pair them off, uncertain which of the younger men was husband of the lovely woman. The old man was probably someone's father.

The bare-chested man began walking about the deck, slapping palms against his belly and exchanging words with half the passengers: the two old women in black dresses, the adolescent couples at the side railing, the men and women back by the cabin. People on the benches were waving to each other, smiling, exchanging sandwiches from their coolers.

"They're all together." Dan spoke his surprise to Marcy.

"Of course. I saw that when they got on."

"But who are they?"

She gave him a puzzled look. "Tourists like us."

"They don't resemble each other. Maybe they're from the same town. A whole village on an outing."

"Why does it matter? They're having a wonderful time."

The man offered peaches and plums to the two blond children. They looked to their mother for permission, and he patted their heads.

The boat pulled up to a dock at its first stop across the lake, a village of whitewashed houses on a green hillside, gardens bright with flowers, sailboats bobbing at a dozen docks. People sat on the grass at the water's edge. The Frenchmen shouted greetings and received greetings in return. The man in cutoffs brought a mock trumpet to his lips and blatted a fanfare; the immaculate man boomed rhythm as he mimed a drum.

The French began shifting places, ordering more beer, passing out food. The two women in black beckoned the old man for cake. The three women who had been behind Dan and Marcy moved to a bench in front of the bare-chested man where Dan could see them clearly. He watched the lovely one closely, sensing what a pleasant person she was, how the others seemed to light up when she gave them a smile. The immaculate man sat beside her and took her hand in both of his. Her husband. Dan's heart sank. But then the man in cutoffs moved to a space on her left and took the other hand.

Dan was surprised at his relief. He didn't want to know who she was married to. It was pleasant to sit there in the breeze and believe she was available, that all he had to do was wait until the two men left and move beside her. She would smile and touch his face as though they had always loved each other. In their hotel, she would undo his brace, stroke fingers across his back, up and down his leg, and he would be healed.

The Frenchmen began singing, rounds, voices from all corners of the deck, at first songs familiar to Dan, like "Fr`ere Jacques," then tunes he had never heard before. The bare-chested man took the lead, standing at the boat's stern and waving arms like a conductor. His voice kept losing the key, but his enthusiasm was infectious. He lifted the blond boy to his shoulders, and the boy mimicked his gestures, two sets of arms leading the music.

Suddenly they all became quiet, except for a pure, crystal soprano that seemed to echo from the lake shore. Dan realized it came from the lovely woman sitting shyly on the bench, hands folded, gazing down at the deck. He felt the tears well in his eyes, let them flow, not caring what Marcy would think or say.

Now the Frenchmen were all singing again, some dancing, the adolescents first, laughing with raucous steps. The wife of the bare-chested man resisted his efforts to pull her up until he began tickling. She slapped at his hands and finally joined him, the two of them hopping from one end of the deck to the other.

When the music turned slow, the immaculate man appeared at their bench and asked Marcy to dance, bowing deep at the waist and extended a hand. Her acceptance surprised Dan, and he wondered what he would do if she sat beside the man when the dance was over.

He didn't watch them, instead fixed his attention on the old man shuffling between the two old women in black. When the woman in shorts sat beside him, he returned her greeting but shook his head and covered his ears to indicate he did not understand her language. She laughed and swirled a hand, indicating that she was inviting him to join the dance. He made an unhappy face and pointed to his brace. "Bad back." He spoke slowly. "Mal back. Hurts much. Pain." When she squinted bewilderment, he took her hand in his and touched it to his brace. He expected her to pull away as if singed; but she patted the hard plastic insert. "So so," she soothed. The lovely woman was looking at them, eyes fixed on her friend's hand. Dan tried to meet her glance.

The bare-chested man stood over them. "Vite, vite," he told Dan. The woman in shorts spoke a long explanation, pointing and touching. The man waved her off, wrapped his arms around Dan and pulled him up. Dan stood so bewildered his pain felt distant and detached.

The Frenchman guided him into the midst of the dancers and called to the immaculate man, who swirled Marcy to a spot directly in front of Dan and then quickly stepped away. They just stared at each other. The bare-chested man arranged them, laughing all the time, placing Dan's right hand on Marcy's waist, his left on her shoulder, wrapped both her hands around Dan's brace. "Faites danser," he commanded.

Dan took the first step, stiff and awkward, his leg cramped, knifepoints stabbing down his hip. But Marcy followed his lead, and they were dancing, turning a circle to the Frenchmen's song, the group backing away to clear a space for them, cheering their efforts. Dan saw the lovely woman's face aglow with a smile. She was so happy for them.

STEF

ALTHOUGH THREE TAXIS WAITED OUTSIDE THE HOTEL, Victor took the tube from Green Park to Earl's Court because that was the way Stephanie would have traveled. She lived on Hentee Crescent, off Warwick Road, her street just a squiggle on his London pocket map.

He checked the address again on the envelope his daughter had used to mail a birthday card two months ago, her first communication in almost a year. "Stef" she had signed in a new printing he didn't recognize. During the time they lived together—he and she and her mother—she was always called Stephanie and wrote her signature in a flourished script.

The card had annoyed him with its magenta flowers smeared on cheap paper under the words "Birthday Wishes." He didn't bother to read the rhymed message, throwing the card out in that night's garbage, unwilling to show it to Julia, to have her hold it at an edge with two fingers and arch a brow. But he had saved the envelope, stuffed it in a desk drawer with scribbled notes and business cards he'd been meaning to enter into a permanent directory.

Victor left the Earl's Court station via the Warwick Road exit, up a ringing metal stairway and past three lavender-haired punks hovering over the ticket machines. On the street he faced the grey front of the exhibition hall, again wondering why everything modern in London was so ugly. Julia wanted to believe London was a city of elegance, nothing but quality shops and glittering restaurants. She refused to notice the soot eaten into the marble facades or the trash trampled in the gutters. He hadn't told her where he was going, even that he knew where Stephanie lived.

He rarely mentioned his daughter to Julia and she never asked. Planning this trip, their first abroad together, he told himself there was no danger of running into Stephanie in the St. James chambers where his meetings would be held. He and Julia would travel in different circles. But that morning as he lay watching Julia's soft breathing beside him, though they had made love during the night, Victor felt he had no more right to touch her sleeping form than he did a stranger's. Before she awoke he left the hotel to look for Stephanie.

She and Arnie had split up. He'd heard that much. Her mother called him at his office whenever she learned another traumatic detail of their daughter's life. He didn't have the heart to tell her he'd rather not know.

At the corner of West Cromwell Road he stood at a traffic light for several minutes while a stream of lorries rumbled by, spewing diesel smoke and clanking chains against their undercarriages. He thought it must be the most unpleasant corner in the city, an intersection of two wide roadways glutted with hulking vehicles. When the light changed, he had to run across to avoid a van that swerved into a right turn.

Victor made several passes up and down the block, finally looking closely at his pocket map. Hentee Crescent didn't join Warwick Road; he could reach it only by cutting through an unnamed alley cluttered with rubbish bins. Though the word crescent had a graceful sound, evoking great sweeps of Georgian town houses, this one was a grimy cluster of squat dark-bricked buildings facing a narrow arc of pavement.

From where he stood he could see through an open window into a barren ground floor room, just a few wooden chairs on a scrap of carpet, the walls papered with a splashy design of oversized flowers that reminded him of the birthday card. Two women in purdah came out onto the front steps, jabbering harsh, throaty sounds. Stephanie's building was three down, identical to the others except for the shrunken white curtains hanging in all the windows. He checked the envelope again, hoping he'd made a mistake.

Only when he pushed back the frosted glass door and stood in the foyer did he consider that she might not be home, that she might be working or shopping or visiting. His daughter's life was a mystery to him now.

A brass wall plate contained narrow slots to identify the tenants, a small black button beside each slot. He expected to find Arnie's surname, but she had used her own—his.

He rang, waited a minute or two, and rang again. This time the inner door buzzed and he turned the knob to step into the hallway.

"Who is it?" Stephanie shouted down the stairwell, suspicious.

"It's your father," he called.

"Oh."

Victor couldn't tell what that sound meant—relief, hostility, indifference?

"Where are you?" he asked her. "Second floor. Up three flights."

Victor climbed slowly. How easy it would be to turn and step back into the street. He averted his eyes from the dark hand marks smeared along the wall.

Stephanie stood in a doorway, an underweight girl wearing baggy ankle-tight jeans and an inside out sweatshirt from her old college, nap showing, the school name meaningless in reverse letters. Her light hair was tangled; the lack of makeup gave her face a blank look. He imagined Julia's judgment: with just a touch of blush and eye shadow she'd be a pretty girl. Stephanie watched him silently, reactionless at this first sight of her father in two years.

"Your card came," he said.

"You didn't have to fly three thousand miles to tell me that."

"It surprised me."

"I was staring at a rack and had an impulse."

"And picked me."

"A coincidence of the calendar. What brings you here?"

"I'm passing through. The first time since I visited during your junior term."

"Before Arnie." Her mouth twisted as if she had more to say. He didn't respond, wouldn't let her provoke him.

"Business this time?"

"Some business. Some pleasure."

"That must mean you're with what's her name."

"Julia."

"If you say so."

"Did your mother tell you about her?"

Stephanie shrugged. "Where is she?"

"Probably shopping for silk scarves."

"But you're not."

"No, I'm visiting my daughter."

She braced a hand on her hip, narrowed her eyes. "Uninvited."

She was trying hard to look furious, but Victor knew it would be all right, no scene. Her threats had always been a bluff—except for Arnie.

"I've heard that Londoners are very hospitable people. Just ring a bell and somebody will offer you a cup of tea."

She turned and moved back into a room, no longer blocking the entrance. He stepped in after her and closed the door.

This wallpaper was terrible too, a repeated pattern of eighteenth-century drawing room scenes, bare-shouldered women in gowns puffed with crinoline, periwigged men, the step of a quadrille, a curtsy, a bow. Whoever had hung the paper hadn't bothered to align the rolls; the room was filled with mismatched people.

Victor sat in an overstuffed chair, sinking with a twang of springs. He rubbed his hands over the threadbare fabric of the armrests. The front windows were closed, large panes vibrating from the lorry rumble on Warwick Road. Stephanie clattered through drawers of a tiny kitchen unit set in an alcove.

Besides the entrance, the room had one other door, closed shut, white enamel chipped down to bare wood. The only furnishings were a sofa even shabbier than the chair, some odd tables, a few throw rugs spread over linoleum, and a thin bookcase stuffed with college texts and warped paperbacks. The prints tacked on the walls were unusual, posters for exhibitions at galleries he had never heard of. Stephanie had always liked art, but these stark prints clashed with the ornate paper.

She filled a pot with water. "It's instant."

"Fine," he said, though he hated instant. "How long have you been living here?"

"Since Arnie. He had it first. Shared with a mate called Sid. Then I came along and poor Sid was out on the street. Arnie too now."

"What happened to him?"

She shrugged. "He turns up now and then. I thought it was him when you rang."

"Are you still friendly?"

She snorted, a mannerism that annoyed him, especially because he suspected she used it often. "With him? He downs four or five pints to build up nerve, then pounds on the door demanding to see his kid."

"Where is the baby?" Victor finally asked, though he'd been searching the room for signs of a child's presence, listening for a gurgle or a cry. Then he recognized the acrid diaper pail odor.

"The baby's name is Margaret."

"I know. Your mother told me."

Stephanie set two cups in their saucers, poured milk in a pitcher. "Since when did you two become so chummy?"

"We're in touch."

"That's news to me. The last I heard you were both ranting."

"We stopped being angry with one another a long time ago."

"Now you have news of my downfall to bring you together."

"We're concerned."

"Isn't it rather late for that?"

Victor stirred his tea, the clink of his spoon the only sound in the room. "Is the baby with a sitter?"

"Sitter? Why no." Stephanie assumed a genteel accent. "Margaret's nanny has taken her for a stroll through the park." Then in her normal voice, "She's having her nap."

"I'd like to see her."

"Granddad." She didn't smile.

"I suppose I am," he said.

Without a word, Stephanie opened the chipped white door and revealed a cluttered room with dark blue walls, a thick mahogany headboard, clothing heaped atop the bed quilt, and upended toys scattered across the floor—stuffed animals, bright plastic balls, dolls. She moved inside where Victor could no longer see her. He leaned forward and gave a start at the sudden wail.

Stephanie cooed. "Did I wake you up, lovey? It's all right. Mummy's here."

The sobbing slowed and quickly stopped, replaced by deep sucking sounds.

"She's wet," Stephanie said. "I have to change her."

Her murmurs were too soft for him to hear now. He saw a small foot kick into his line of vision, then disappear, heard a giggle.

Stephanie stepped back into the front room carrying a frail looking child with fine honey-colored hair and a large forehead. The baby stared at him through round blue eyes and drew on the pacifier that obscured her mouth. The skin struck him as too pale, the arms brittle.

"When was she six months?" Victor asked, wondering if he should offer to hold the baby.

"She isn't. Three weeks from now."

"She looks well-behaved."

"You've only seen her for ten seconds."

"Does she give you problems?"

"She's a baby, isn't she."

"I only meant that some are easier than others."

"So are some parents."

Victor clutched the armrests and dug fingers into the chair's padding, then pushed himself up until he was standing. When he approached them, the baby shrank against Stephanie's shoulder with a look of distress. The pacifier dropped to the floor. He expected bawling. But the baby just gazed at him with puzzlement when he stooped to retrieve the plastic ring.

"Should I wash it?" he asked.

"You have to be immune to germs to survive around here."

He reached the nipple out toward the baby's face and watched her mouth close around it. Her palm, small and warm, rested on his knuckles. He held his hand under her touch until Stephanie hoisted the padded backside and broke the contact.

"Is she healthy?" he asked. "She looks so thin."

"I feed her." Stephanie glared.

"I didn't mean that."

"She gets colds. We see the National Health doctor. But I think she picks up more bugs sitting in the waiting room with so many other kids."

"   You can use the health services?"

"Of course."

"What's your status here?"

"I'm on the dole. The Council pays for this flat. A bedraggled social worker stops by now and then to fill out a form and then I get my charity. After all, I'm a Brit's mum." She bounced the baby with an exaggerated rhythm, chanting, "Margaret, Margaret, subject of the Queen."

Does Arnie help?" He expected the snort this time, didn't know why he had bothered to ask the question.

"Arnie's only good for one thing. The first time I saw him in that pub I knew. I didn't care if he had two bob in his pocket or could speak a complete sentence. And my instinct was right. For six months he was spectacular. Then we had an accident"—she held the child out at arm's length. "Somehow he was under the impression that if you stopped afterwards it would make the mistake unhappen."

"He doesn't sound like a mental giant."

"Arnie was the highpoint of my junior year abroad. Everybody else went home to be seniors. I stayed on for independent study . . . Being Margaret's mother." She sang the words, then tossed the baby and nuzzled her cheek.

"Is it worth it?" His eyes scanned the room.

"Margaret, are you worth it?" The baby's mouth pulled at the pacifier. "And how's your life?" she asked Victor. "You didn't pick up Julia in a pub."

Although Victor said nothing, she held up a hand to silence him. "Don't tell me. She's witty, elegant, sensual, and very well dressed. All her undies are in Burberry plaid."

"Exactly right." He couldn't help smiling. "Except for the plaid. Though she may be buying those right now."

"Does she know you're seeing your ne'er-do-well daughter?"

"Yes," he lied.

"I suppose hers are models of elegance and grace."

"Sons. Two of them, both in college."

"They'll never be permitted a junior year abroad."

"In fact, the older one will be here next term."

"Be sure to have him look me up. Sample some local color."

"It won't be his first visit."

"I should have guessed a classy woman like Julia would be well traveled. How does she stack up against my mother?"

"They're very different."

"In whose favor?"

"Julia is much more at ease with the world. Your mother is a shy woman."

"And you've always wanted someone with style."

"Only if there's substance."

"Poor Granddad." She spoke to the baby, looking down where the drooling had left a dark circle on the reversed sweatshirt. "Disappointed by wife and daughter. We could live in Mayfair with what he spent on country day schools. No tuition too high in his quest for the ideal offspring. All he got for his money were bad reports—'Stephanie has a rebellious streak.'"

"The euphemism was 'high spirits.'"

"Exactly what Arnie found so fascinating." She cradled the baby and rocked her from side to side. "Will you and Julia marry?"

"Unlikely."

"Maybe you should adopt her."

"She's fine the way she is. We're perfect together in small doses."

"Before reality can intrude its ugly head . . . the reason you and Mother divorced."

"What reality?"

"Arnie." She touched the tip of her nose to the baby's. "Grandma and Grandpa couldn't bear having a daughter who bedded down with a common navvy. So they punished each other by getting divorced."

"It didn't happen that way. The only thing you changed was our timing. We'd planned to wait until you graduated."

"Well, thank you for wanting to shelter your little girl from life's cruelties."

Victor's blood surged. "You enjoyed rubbing our faces in Arnie!" "At least he pretended to love me!"

Her face flushed, nostrils quivering, eyes glazed with tears. The baby, frightened, burst out crying.

He reached out toward the child, but Stephanie swung away from him, clutching her daughter tightly. She pretended to study one of the prints, a dark semi-human shape with swirl of black ink for a face.

Victor sat again, on the sofa this time. "Why do you sign yourself Stef now?"

For a moment he thought she wouldn't answer. Then she said, "That was Arnie's name for me."

"But you're not with Arnie anymore."

She turned toward him, approached the sofa. "It's more appropriate for somebody on the dole." He thought she would weep and quickly stood up beside her.

Her head hung and her hair fell limply over her eyes. He wanted to push the hair back, to close both hands over the bones of her face. But she just swallowed hard and pressed her mouth to the baby's head.

Victor remembered his rage when she called about Arnie and dropping out of school, how he had cursed her name and smashed down the receiver. Now her vulnerability made him feel ashamed.

"May I hold her?" he asked after a silence.

"It's Arnie's daughter you know."

"That's not her fault. We don't choose our parents."

"And we're stuck with our children."

He held out his arms.

"She's wet again," Stephanie said.

She passed the child to him and at once he felt the warm dampness seeping through the cloth of her playsuit. The baby squirmed in his unfamiliar arms, face trembling at the verge of collapse. Then he recalled a lesson Stephanie's mother had given him when their daughter was an infant: hold a baby tightly, tuck it firm against your chest, let it feel your heartbeat. When he did, the child calmed, rested her head against his throat. Her hair smelled of sour milk; she needed a bath. Wet and stinking, his granddaughter.

"Margaret," he said, testing the name, and again, "Margaret," making it a soothing sound.

He pictured Margaret where they once had lived, the tiny fingers touching flower petals, the blue eyes entranced by the ducks on the pond.

"She usually doesn't take to strangers," Stephanie said.

"You could go home," he told her, his middle knotting with anxiety even as he spoke. "Finish college. Other girls with babies do it."

"You used to say London is the most interesting city in the world."

"Not this way. Not when you live on Hentee Crescent."

"Thanks for the offer. But I'll stay where I am."

"For God's sake, why? There's plenty of money. You know that."

He had spoken too loudly, made agitated sounds. The baby stiffened, drew away, and began to whimper. Stephanie lifted her from him, smacking kisses until the child was cooing again.

"I made my choices," she said, "and here I am."

"That's nonsense. We're free to change our lives."

"I haven't worked out this one yet."

He lifted a hand and watched himself hold it poised out in front of him. He saw that she was watching too. All he had to do was touch her and make himself say, I want you back.

"Do one thing for me," she asked suddenly.

"What?"

"Bring your friend Julia to dinner some night. Let her sample the native cuisine."

Victor looked to the doorway as if Julia were poised on the threshold for his answer, adjusting white gloves, one finger at a time. "She may have plans."

"She doesn't know you're here, does she?" "No."

Margaret stroked her mother's cheek as if fascinated by the feel of her. Stephanie cupped her hand over the baby's fingertips and looked hard at her father.

"All right." Victor nodded, already dreading the evening. "I'll bring her."

For the first time Stephanie smiled at him.

WHAT EAMON DID

FOR A MOMENT CARTER THOUGHT HE WAS STANDING at the end of the earth, alone on a dirt path on a bluff above the water gazing out at three island shapes in the mist below, and beyond them nothing but a dark sea fading back into the horizon. When he turned his head, he saw houses and stone walls scattered far behind him, the small square automobiles close beside the buildings looking as ancient as the boulders strewn across the landscape. He felt he was the only thing alive as he stepped slowly, boots grinding into the earth. Even the sheep far across a distant field were immobile, still white lumps. Then he saw two figures approaching in the distance, emerging from the dazzling haze of sunset. Carter knew they were human, erect, but moving with odd gaits. As they neared, he could see that one of them stabbed the ground with a walking stick. It was a woman, a tiny, old, curved-backed woman barely taller than her stick. And beside her, her hand clutching his elbow, a young man in a grey suit and tie who stumbled forward with each step, arms rigid, right foot coming down hard but only the toe of the left touching the earth. He looked straight ahead with a glaring stare. Carter spoke a greeting as they passed. The man ignored him as if he were invisible, and he couldn't tell whether the woman nodded or was just bobbing her head. He stopped and watched them until they disappeared around a bend in the path.

•

For the first time in weeks he felt an urge to seek human conversation. Usually he walked alone, hours each day across remote fields, buying food in a local shop, spending the midafternoon sprawled out on rocks or on the moist green soil reading a book, some ragged paperback that he had found abandoned in a bus station or in one of the bed and breakfasts where he stayed when the rain was too heavy to sleep outside. Reading was a diversion, but he never choose a book, preferring to take whatever came his way, random words on a page. The days were long in summer, and he sought most the sense of endless time that required nothing of him.

•

On the best days he could even forget this feeling of freedom was only an illusion, rationed to a few weeks in July and August with money always a problem, each expense entered in a notebook and immediately subtracted from his daily allotment. When that ran out, no matter how hungry or thirsty he was, he allowed himself nothing more. Some nights, chill in a field, wrapped from chin to toes in the single blanket he carried, he would chew the sweet damp clover grass and swallow it like a grazing animal.

•

The rest of the year Carter lived in a two-room flat in a crowded city neighborhood an ocean away, most of his furniture collected from curb sides or passed on by the janitors in his school, stiff wooden chairs, paint-chipped shelves, grey filing cabinets with twisted drawers where he stored his changes of clothes. Even at home he kept a running tab of expenses, obsessed with saving enough for his summer airfare and the cost of days in this empty green countryside.

•

He taught hostile twelve-year-olds, who by the time they had reached the seventh grade despaired of any future beyond furtive pleasures and the grind for subsistence. Every fall each new group repeated the same strategies for rebellion—dropped books, belches, obscene figures on the blackboard, firecrackers. But when they saw that Carter didn't care enough to be angry, they took no pleasure from their defiance and passed the periods in sullen boredom while Carter droned on and never bothered to learn who they were, calling them by the name of whichever past student they reminded him of.

•

Once he had worked at a desk in his own office, well paid for making decisions and devising plans. He received promotions and bonuses. But he hated listening to the others at lunches and meetings, all so serious about whatever project was at hand, craving recognition and advancement, ridiculous in their quests for picayune victories. For a quarter of his salary he found a school where he could teach without an education degree and kill the time between each summer escape.

His wife left when he stopped being an executive: "How can you do this to me?" But he knew she would leave anyway, sooner or later, that she would realize it was no life for her with a man who wanted to live like a stone in a field.

•

Even though he took the book from his pack and tried to read, he could not stop remembering the stare of the man on the path. The spine of this paperback had been folded a hundred times, twisted so much that chunks of pages had fallen out. The gaps made this book nothing but disconnected fragments that ended in a mid-sentence limbo. But now the words seemed to slide off the paper, and Carter saw nothing but those dark fixed eyes.

Of course, he understood the actuality, that the pair were mother and son, that the man was not a boy but a person of his age, the flesh of his face starting to sink, lines forming around the mouth. And he knew the man had not been arrogant in his snub. This country did not hide its defectives. In the cities he passed through on the way to more open land he saw people with hunchbacks and goiters and open malignancies eating into faces. But this man troubled him more than any of the others in his fierce isolation.

•

As the sun began to set behind the shapes of the three islands, Carter shivered even though this was a warm evening. Unwilling to stay alone in a field, he walked the three miles into the village, rented a room for the night, and went out to the main street where people were strolling past the shop windows, studying the menus outside a small restaurant. A small hotel displayed a hand lettered poster by the main entrance—"Single's Night." From a window that opened to the sidewalk Carter could see inside to a bare room where four middle-aged couples fox-trotted on a pale wood floor to a recording of a song he remembered from childhood.

•

Carter turned onto the one side street, a road that curved downhill and led out of the village into farmland. Mid-block he saw a squat stone building apart from the others with the sign "Tavern" over a wood plank door. Though he was not a tall man, he had to stoop to step inside.

It was a low windowless room with dark beams and a grey partition in the middle that stopped abruptly before the bar at the back. The light was so dim, the air so heavy with cigarette smoke, that he had to blink and stand a few moments until he could see. All the tables were filled, on one side of the partition old men in black caps gazing down into glasses of thick dark liquid, saying very little to each other, the others nodding when anyone did. All the noise was coming from the other side.

Carter stepped over boots and outstretched legs to approach the bar. Someone had printed the word "Music" on a slate hanging next to the mirror. A boy no older than his students drew Carter a drink from the tap, tilting the glass, scraping off the head with a flat stick. Carter reached for the glass, but the boy snatched it back to top it off, giving Carter a snide look. Carter dropped coins on a yellow mat, turned, sipped, and leaned back against the bar.

From there he could see the source of the noise, people jammed at a dozen tables, courting couples in the corner, a group of well-dressed grey-haired ladies, obviously tourists, families of several generations, mothers with babies on their laps, young men in work clothes. They were shouting to one another, teasing the lovers, toasting the tourists.

Now Carter could see that every wall in the tavern was covered with postcards, each one pinned to the plaster with a thumbtack in the middle of the top edge. He stepped forward and bent over a table to look more closely at the cards directly in front of him. They came from all over—Greece, Spain, Belgium, Miami, Los Angeles. Without lifting them to read the messages, he was sure they were sent by the locals on their holidays, and as he glanced about the room, couldn't imagine people like these traveling so far from home. Then it struck him that at the end of this summer he could send his own card addressed just to the tavern in this village. He had no idea what message he would write on the back of a photo of a city he hated. Of course, no one would know who the writer was; no one would remember an anonymous stranger from a single evening.

•

He heard clapping, a sudden murmur, and followed glances to see two men enter through a side door just beyond the alcove with the toilets. They were the musicians, one carrying a small wooden pipe, the other a concertina. People greeted them by name, reached out and squeezed their arms as they passed—"Nick, Terry." The piper answered for them both, "Good to see you," in a rough, hoarse voice. He must have been Nick, a thickset man in a blue denim jacket with dark brows, deep eyes, and a sparse dark beard that grew high up his cheekbones. The man with the concertina, Terry, was pink and round-faced, skin so smooth he looked as if he never shaved. He wore a constant smile, but Nick seemed very serious, neck muscles taut, his pipe looking fragile amid the knuckles of large, hairy hands.

They sat on two empty chairs against the front wall. Someone handed Terry a glass of stout, but Nick only Schweppes and a lemon slice. Almost immediately they filled the room with raucous, lilting music. People began drumming feet against the stone floor, swaying heads, tapping tabletops. They were all smiling. Carter knew they would have leapt up and danced if there had been room in the tavern. He might have danced himself if he knew how.

•

Carter stopped slapping his hand on his thigh to watch a family enter the room, tiptoeing through the crowd against the partition, a pale, freckled little man with a puff of red hair, a small boy who looked just like him, and a dumpy young woman with a round, blank face carrying a baby sleeping on her shoulder. The man wore a dark brown suit that was too tight for him, short in the arms and legs, all three jacket buttons fastened over a tan sweater. The woman's cotton dress seemed faded, too cold for the night air. The boy had on a tie and jacket over dungarees. No one else paid attention to them, as if deliberately pretending they did not notice. Still tiptoeing, the man passed into the alcove and retrieved three folding chairs for his family. All through their entry, the unfolding and the sitting, the musicians played more loudly, wildly, Nick the piper stamping a foot and bouncing up and down in his seat.

The crowd cheered when they finished the tune. Even the old men in black were nodding. Nick studied his pipe, took out a handkerchief and wiped it very carefully, held it up to the dim bulb in the ceiling lamp and squinted one eye. Terry played a scale as if he could not keep his fingers still.

Then Nick looked straight at the little man and smiled; but Carter could see that it was more a twisting of his mouth, the straggly hair of his mustache sticking straight out, the grey fillings of his molars exposed. "Well, if it isn't Eamon," Nick said. "Out with the family on a night like this. And how are you, Eamon?" The voice rumbled, and Carter thought of all the stones in the fields.

Eamon, the little man, stared down at the floor and squirmed on the folding chair. His wife flushed and hugged the baby. The boy folded his hands and sat stiffly.

"It's always a great treat to see Eamon," Nick continued as if address-ing an audience. "Isn't it great, Terry?" Terry nodded and sounded a long drawn chord, though Carter could tell he wanted Nick to stop.

Carter glanced at the boy behind the bar for a clue. This taunting seemed so unlikely, that a timid person like Eamon could have done some-thing to annoy a man like Nick. Of course, they both could have grown up in this village, with Eamon the butt of ridicule since childhood, Nick's scorn an empty repetition of an old routine. Carter saw it in his class-room every year, one boy singled out as the butt, blamed for all misdeeds, evoking snickers each time the roll was called. But here no one else was participating, the tourists bewildered, the locals pretending to ignore it. Whatever had happened was between Nick and Eamon.

"Are you being good, Eamon?"

Terry pressed the concertina into a sound like a long sigh and then slid into a tune. Nick had to follow along, still half rising and pointing the pipe toward Eamon every time he played a high note. Eamon sat in silence, saying nothing, not ordering drinks, but giving his son a coin for a soda when the boy poked his side and whispered. Nick tooted a rhythm that followed the boy's shy steps to the bar, then leered at Eamon.

•

Carter was surprised that the mystery intrigued him. For all his summers in this country, he didn't know the people beyond a few brief conversations with people on buses and landladies, talk of weather and the outrageous prices. He had chosen this place for the landscape, the empty miles beyond the sight of any cottage, the stones, the layers of carbonized moss, the abandoned remnants of ancient habitation that suddenly appeared in the middle of nowhere. At night, alone in a field beneath distant stars, he felt a pure sensation of unremitting time, the insignificance of all that people allowed to obsess their lives. But now he was curious. What had Eamon done?

If what he did had been so awful, why was he here? He must have known Nick was performing this night. So why did he dress in his best suit and bring his family to hear him take abuse? Why was he so passive about it? Perhaps he felt so guilty that he was punishing himself with public shame. But to look at Eamon you'd think he was absolutely harmless, the most innocuous man in the world.

Carter had an eye for malevolence after so many years of teaching twelve-year-olds. On the first day of class he could spot the really nasty ones, boy or girl, no matter how seemingly sweet the expression, the ones who would do something cruel or corrupt before the year was over. But all he saw in Eamon was weakness, a man too craven to risk breaking a rule.

•

Even though he was exceeding his day's allotment, Carter signaled the boy bartender and ordered another drink. "Do you know that man in the suit?"

"Eamon? He's from the village."

"What does he do?"

"Works in a shop."

"Why does Nick hate him so much?"

The boy turned and plunged dirty glasses into a sink. "You'd have to ask Nick about that."

•

No one would tell him, Carter was sure. Perhaps only Nick and Eamon themselves, and why would they speak to a stranger? But he could try if he had an opportunity, though not now with the music so feverish, Nick piping with one hand and wiping his brow with the other, rubbing the handkerchief across the mat of chest hair showing from his open fl annel shirt. Only Eamon and his family were not caught up in the rhythm, Eamon gazing fixedly as if he did not hear a sound. Now and then Nick would meet his eyes and wink.

Carter looked to the wife, Mrs. Eamon, for a clue. Perhaps Nick had seduced her or she had thrown herself on Nick in a moment of crazed passion. But she was so bland, so lethargic that he couldn't imagine Nick bothering or she having the spirit to act out her most secret desires. Unless Nick had seduced her for revenge. But that would have been a response to something that Eamon did, a gesture, not the root cause.

•

At the end of the tune, Nick began again. "Eamon, my boy. And how's life treating you, Eamon?"

Carter looked hard at Nick, trying to force his attention across the room, a recognition that would give him a sign. But when the man finally responded, in the instant he locked on, the eyes were hard and unyielding.

"Eamon, you're looking a bit peaked. Are you sleeping the way you should?"

•

Carter wondered what would happen if he bought Eamon a drink, a pint for the man and one for his wife. But they wouldn't have been able to talk, not with the music resounding through the tavern. People had to shout to comment to whoever sat next to them; he could see their mouths wide open, the lips forming sounds.

Then Eamon stood up and walked into the alcove with the toilets. For a few seconds Carter stayed at the bar, stunned by the sudden movement, before he followed.

They stood side by side at a urinal that took up one wall, a water tank above at the ceiling connected by gleaming copper pipes. Carter hadn't realized how badly he needed relief.

"How do you like the music?" he asked.

"It's what they do around here," Eamon said. It was the first time Carter had heard the man speak. The voice was soft and sullen, as if begrudging the words.

"Then you must live in the village."

Eamon nodded.

"And know the musicians."

He nodded again.

"What do you think of the piper?"

"He's been playing all his life."

"He must be a friend of yours then."

"The man's no friend of mine"

Eamon zipped up quickly and turned to leave. Carter knew he would have to speak quickly and began talking about a subject he hadn't allowed to enter his thoughts all day.

"You wouldn't think my daughter's getting married tomorrow, would you?"

Eamon gave him a strange look. "Congratulations," he said in a tone that made it clear he did care.

"It's on the other side of the ocean, so I won't be there. Her sisters will and her brother, and her mother. She wanted me to come. My daughter, not her mother. Her mother wouldn't give me a hand if I were drowning in front of her. My daughter called me before I flew over here. But I couldn't afford another round trip. It's hard to make exceptions when you have just enough money to live. It's only a formality anyway. Part of the show to have a father give her away. She's getting a husband. What does she need with a father anyway?"

"I guess so," Eamon said and reached out a hand to push the door.

Carter seized his arm. "Why does that man hate you?" But Eamon shook him off and plunged back into the room.

•

Carter splashed water on his face, rubbed at his eyes with his thumbs. The towel roll had reached his end, hanging half loose and filthy with hand smears. He had to wipe his face on a shirt sleeve.

When he went back to the bar, the musicians were standing as they played, sounding solo bursts and answering each other with a rapid tempo that got faster with each note of the tune. People were cheering, urging them on. The two of them kicked their chairs over and started threading through the crowded tables, playing and dancing, bringing the tavern to a pitch of excitement. Even the boy behind the bar was laughing now, beating a wash bucket with a wooden spoon.

Nick led Terry past the edge of the partition to the old men finally smiling and nodding their heads to the rhythm. Nick paused to drain a full glass of stout in one long swallow, and Terry gave him a look.

When they turned back to the other side of the partition, they had to pass right in front of Eamon's chair, and Carter expected something to happen. Nick seemed to ignore the man, but then stopped abruptly, backstepped, and swirled to face Eamon's wife. "What a night, eh darling? What a night to be married to a great man like Eamon."

In a second she was on her feet, thrusting the baby onto Eamon's lap. The baby was screaming, and she was shrieking, beating at Nick's shoulders, ripping the pipe from his hands and hitting the top of his head with it.

Two of the old men pinned her arms, stronger than she was no matter how she twisted and tried to kick at them. Terry took the pipe from her. But Nick was on the floor, shaking with laughter. "Oh, Eamon, my boy, what a hellfire you've got."

Eamon picked up the baby and dragged the boy by the wrist, heading toward the door of the tavern. The old men pushed his wife after him. When the door opened, Carter could see that it was dark outside, only a few stars visible in the black sky. The door closed quickly, and the room turned silent.

"The entertainment is over," Nick said as he picked himself up and studied his pipe for damage. "And the air is clearer in here. We can play some serious music."

•

Carter left, impelled by an urgent need to get away from the din. Out on the sidewalk, shivering in the chill air, he was sorry he had left his jacket in his backpack. Eamon and his family had disappeared, perhaps had already shut themselves inside their home in the small cluster of the village.

Carter would never learn what the man had done. But whatever it was—some crime or sin or stupid error—it would always matter. People like Nick wouldn't ever let him forget. And Eamon would never leave this village; he would stay in constant humiliation. What good would it do for him to leave? He would always be haunted. He would live out his life in this insignificant place where he had committed an act of great consequence.

Carter turned back toward the main street, wondering if he would recognize the house where he had rented a room for the night, then realized that he didn't want to find it, that he didn't want to be here.

He would retrieve his backpack in the morning. Now he went out into the darkness. Away from the village, back on the path he had walked at sunset, Carter sensed that he was following the maimed footsteps of the man led by his ancient mother, out in a ritual of aimless exercise, not even knowing where he was or why he was.

THE BEAUTIES OF PARIS

As TAYLOR AND HIS DAUGHTER, Ariel, emerged through the Nothing to Declare door into the Charles de Gaulle arrival hall, he saw the driver, a little man with a pointed face and a hat three sizes too big, holding a cardboard printed with Taylor's name. When Taylor said he had to get euros, the driver took their luggage and, in memorized English, asked Taylor to meet him at pickup area 8. Instead of staying with her father, Ariel followed the man, one step behind, like a child, even though she was a woman in her thirties. In line for the cash dispenser, Taylor watched the driver pull a suitcase with each hand, the top of his hat at a level with Ariel's shoulders.

Three American businessmen clustered at the machine, paying more attention to their conversion than the buttons they had to push. Taylor almost said something, fidgeting with the notion that his daughter might run off with the little man and leave him stranded. But he swallowed his impatience, knew he was upset because he and Ariel had been seated rows apart on the crowded flight. He couldn't remember their last real conversation, if there had ever really been one, and he had anticipated seven hours to ease the tension before they got to Paris.

Finally stuffing a thousand euros into his wallet, he saw the sign for area 8 and walked quickly toward it and found himself blocked by a thick crowd coming the other way. He tried to squirm through, but a young woman in an airport uniform stopped him, signaling that he couldn't go ahead. "What's happening?" he asked in English, and a voice behind him answered, "Something about a bomb scare."

"Wonderful," Taylor sighed. It was a mistake, a colossal mistake, coming to Paris, bringing Ariel, as if time in another city would fix things. And now, according to the news, French students were protesting some law about jobs. Had some of them planted explosives? He didn't know what to expect.

Taylor had booked the arrangements six weeks before, shortly after Ariel's mother, his ex-wife, died. Ariel had cared for her, moving back to the room of her childhood for the final months of dreadful pain. The trip was his sister's idea, almost a demand. "Your daughter needs a treat after what she's been through." "Even with me?" he had said. "Even with you," his sister had told him, tight-lipped.

Calling to make the offer, he expected Ariel to refuse, especially after many seconds of silence, but when she spoke, it was "Yes," just the one word. Taylor had responded quickly, "It will be good for you to get away." He could almost hear her nodding, and she had said, "I'd like to get away." He had hoped for more enthusiasm, then realized she was just as apprehensive about spending time with him as he was to be alone with her.

Outside the terminal at area 6, Taylor realized a path to 8 was clear. He saw Ariel standing beside a yellow van, tall and thin, stoop shouldered, her face long and narrow, like his. Ever since she had been a teenager, he sensed she blamed him for her face. Despite the resemblance, he felt he was looking at a stranger. He knew she saw him, but she didn't gesture. It was a young woman emerging from the passenger door who did, plump and little with close-cropped hair. Taylor assumed she was the driver's daughter. Two fathers, two daughters.

Once he was belted on the bench seat beside Ariel. The young woman turned to him. "We go now."

"What about the protests?" Taylor asked her. "Will we be able to get into the museums and monuments?"

When she gave him a blank look, he tried again using remnants of his college French: "Voulez nous visit les monuments y des musee? Avec les protester contre de law?"

She smiled and shook her head in bewilderment.

"Stop it," Ariel said, her voice sharp, the first time she had spoken since they got off the plane. "You're not making any sense."

"At least I'm amusing her. The stupid American she can talk about to friends."

When the van pulled off a highway onto a city street, Taylor craned for a street sign and took out his map. He liked tracing routes, hoping to find the way to their hotel. For several blocks he was lost, then located Faubourg St. Antoine in grids F26-27, a nondescript avenue that could have existed in a dozen cities. At first he was eager to show Ariel, but when he saw that she was staring straight at the driver's hat, said nothing.

With the turn onto Avenue Ledru Rollin, he knew exactly where they were, heading directly toward Pont d'Austerlitz to cross onto the Left Bank. But at the intersection with Rue de Lyon, a group of what looked like fourteen-year-olds, mostly boys, mostly dark skinned, swarmed over the street, blocking traffic, chanting and pumping their fists. The cars ahead of them turned away, but their driver—to Taylor's surprise—chose to go straight ahead. "What are you doing?" he said and could see Ariel cowering, hunched forward, her arms pressed tight across her chest.

The driver stopped when the children surrounded the van. Two boys with wool ski caps pulled down to their eyebrows suddenly slid back the door on Taylor's side, exposing him. They shouted something he did not understand, and he tensed, expecting them to pull him out onto the street. When they hesitated, he slammed the door closed, gripping the handle and leaning his weight into it.

Other boys popped open the driver's door and stuck their heads inside. The driver nodded and blew the horn, again and again. The children let out a cheer, backing off from the van and waving. They parted to let the driver creep through, slapping hands on the van's metal.

Taylor sat back, wiping sweat from his forehead with the sleeve of his jacket. "They're just kids," he said. "Playing at being protesters. Harmless." He hoped Ariel would nod, but her jaw was clenched.

When they crossed Pont d'Austerlitz, he pointed to the sign for the Jardin des Plantes and tried speaking to her again. "Remember when you were here as a little girl?" Twenty-four years ago, he quickly calculated. "You wanted to come back to the zoo every day we were in Paris. The lions and tigers fascinated you. The big cats."

"But we only went once."

"Your mother took you shopping instead."

"She still had some of the silk scarves she bought. In a drawer. I don't think she ever wore them."

"People are like that," Taylor said. "They consider some possessions too good to use."

"Then they die."

"Maybe actually wearing them would have been a disappointment." He didn't know why he said that.

"Mother had more than enough to disappoint her." Ariel almost whispered the words, as if she didn't want to be overheard by the driver and the young woman who might have been the man's daughter.

Before Taylor could think of a response, the van double-parked in front of their hotel, the driver jumping out to raise the back hatch and unload their suitcases onto the sidewalk. Taylor over tipped the little man, a twenty euro note, the smallest bill from the money machine, relieved to have gotten this far. With a "Merci, monsieur," the man was back in the van and gone, the vehicle vanished around a corner.

Taylor held the door so that Ariel could enter the small lobby first. Because he wanted to be on the Left Bank near quaint Rue Mouffetard and the cafes of Place de la Contrescarpe, he had found a web site that recommended this small three-star hotel on Rue Monge, a working class avenue lined with shops, a tiny plumbing supply store on one side of the hotel and a laundry on the other.

Once registered, they crowded their luggage into a narrow elevator up to rooms on the third floor. Ariel's was across from his, facing the street. When she unlocked the door, he saw how small her room was, barely enough space to maneuver around the bed to the wardrobe.

"Do you want to take a nap?" he asked her.

"I'm exhausted. I need a shower."

He suggested they meet for dinner at seven, four hours away. He would call for her. She shut the door and bolted it. Taylor kicked off his shoes and stretched out on his own bed, his eyes burning, unable to sleep. His room seemed even smaller than his daughter's, the walls closing in. He turned on the TV and clicked through channels until he found BBC news, not paying attention until the screen showed pictures of the demonstrations in Paris, store windows smashed and a car smoldering on its side. But that was on the other side of the city, far away.

Taylor propped himself up on two pillows and tried to imagine how he would talk to his daughter, how to start a conversation. Ariel had been barely a teenager when he divorced her mother, off to college a few years later and then to a job several hundred miles from where he had ended up. When she was young, they saw each other only a few times a year after he drove hours for a meal in a restaurant, neutral territory, Ariel stealing glances at her watch, checking how long it would be before her mother came to get her. Taylor couldn't understand how his daughter could live with the woman, the way she had let herself go, the house a disaster.

But he knew better than to criticize, asking meaningless questions about school, eager for signs of the infant he had been thrilled to hold.

During the period of his second marriage, they didn't have much contact, not after Ariel's initial reaction to Carolyn, only ten years older than her, an attractive woman whose manic need for entertainment eventually exhausted Taylor. He had never known the men in Ariel's life, not even the one named James during her brief engagement. Ariel hadn't been lucky with men. He remembered looking at her when she was an adolescent and realizing that she wasn't attractive. No one will love her, he told himself then, immediately guilty for the thought. Every time the memory came back to him, he felt ashamed.

Taylor had visited Paris a number of times since that first trip with Ariel and her mother, twice with Carolyn and later on his own, more fond of the city with each visit. He had hoped his adult daughter would fall in love with it too, the two of them sharing its treasures, their days filled with conversations about art and architecture, food and wine. A closeness would emerge. But now that he was here, shut into this room with a tiny window that overlooked a tar roof, he didn't know how to begin.

After an hour of staring at a framed poster on the wall, a famous one by an artist whose name he couldn't remember, Taylor gave up trying to sleep. He took a long hot shower and then shaved, wiping the steamed mirror with the edge of his hand again and again. But his reflection kept disappearing in a mist. Even in clean clothes he didn't feel refreshed. He sat on the edge of his bed, watching the minute hand of his travel alarm till it was exactly seven and he could knock on Ariel's door.

She wasn't hungry and didn't want a drink.

"Airplane food?" he asked.

She nodded. "I don't have any appetite. It was a rotten flight. I felt cramped into that window seat."

"You've got long legs." Taylor regretted the words as soon as he spoke them. Her height was another thing she didn't like about herself, though for her generation it wasn't unusual. "I wish we could have sat together."

"I tried to sleep the whole flight."

"Did you?"

"Not at all." She shook her head.

"What about now?"

"It takes me a while to get used to a new bed."

Across Rue Monge, Taylor noticed a dual stairway leading up to Rue Rollin. "How do you feel about a climb?"

She shrugged. "You know this city."

His legs ached and he had to rub his thighs at the halfway landing. Ariel gave the hint of smile. It was the first time he had seen her amused. "I'm showing my age," he said.

After a quick right and then left, they came to Rue Descartes, a narrow street lined with restaurants. Taylor had eaten at several one or two trips ago, recalled the photos of celebrities on the white stone wall inside La Maison de Verlaine, on the ground floor of a building the poet had once lived in, and decades later, Hemingway. In the picture directly across from his table, Jack and Jackie Kennedy and Lyndon and Lady Bird Johnson stood together smiling at the camera. Bang, he had kept thinking. Bang, you're dead.

At the corner of Rue Clovis, Taylor recognized the dome of the Pantheon illuminated by spotlights. Groups of students walked on both sides of the street, chatting happily, at ease with each other, no signs of a protest. A block ahead, a long line waited outside a door to the Sorbonne. Maybe it was over, he thought. But when they got to the front of the Pantheon, he saw three police wagons with their engines running and a street blocked off by metal barriers, policemen with submachine guns posted at the intersection. They wore blue jackets with the word "Police" in large letters across the backs.

"What happened to gendarme?" he asked Ariel.

"Globalization."

He laughed, too loud he realized, but pleased that his daughter had made a joke. Taylor walked on, led the way, paying no attention to street signs, just turning when he saw a building that interested him. He tried to think of comments he could make to his daughter, but nothing seemed right. Finally, he asked her, "How are your shoes?"

"Fine. My shoes are fine." She spoke sharply, as if his question had been an insult.

It was dark now, a faint glow of moonlight emerging whenever the cloud cover thinned. Streetlights and shop windows illuminated their path. Taylor found he had taken them to a broad avenue, Boulevard Saint Michel he discovered from a sign, though he wouldn't have recognized it so empty of people and traffic. To their right, on the other side of a green, he saw the imposing shape of a large building wall, a row of pointed parapets at the roof line, totally dark inside. He paused to check his map but found no indication of what it was. Ariel wouldn't know, of course, and he didn't want to admit his ignorance.

"I'm hungry," she said in a tone that implied he should have known.

"Good idea." Taylor realized he was hungry too, but he didn't see any place that served food, walking toward bright lights two blocks ahead, relieved that a brasserie faced the jets of a large fountain across the boulevard. Inside, only one customer, a young man in a grey overcoat, hunched over the bar.

"Is this all right?"

"Yes, yes. Any place. I want to sit."

He pulled back the door for Ariel and picked a table against the far wall covered with a mirror. His chair faced it. "Carte. Menu, sil vous plait," Taylor asked the bartender, a dark round man with a bald head and a moustache. Behind the bar, a boy of about twelve watched closely as the man handed them laminated cards. The boy was shaped like the man, had the same face. Father and son. Ariel wanted a glass of red wine. Taylor chose a beer, a Stella.

When his drinks came and he ordered an omelet, Ariel a sandwich, he lifted his glass in a toast. "Here's to our days in Paris."

She took a sip of her wine and nodded.

After a few silent minutes, he blurted the topic he had been pondering since the plane ride, forgetting the lines he had rehearsed in his head, and just said, "Would you like to talk about your mother?"

"Why would I want to do that?"

"You've been through a terrible ordeal with her."

"Do you really care? You didn't know her anymore."

"I did once. Nobody should have to face a death like that. Nobody should have to witness it."

"She was my mother."

Taylor groped for a way to change the subject.

The door from the street opened, and in the mirror he saw the bartender and his son look up from their newspaper, the young man bolt off his stool and hurry to a young woman the moment she stepped inside, enfolding her in an embrace, the wide sleeves of his overcoat wrapped around her back. Holding her close, he guided her to a table, and the bartender followed with his glass.

When they were seated, the young man leaned forward and gripped both her hands in his, his mouth close to her ear, whispering something. Taylor could see that the man was very handsome, a classic French face under dark curls. The young woman had her back to the mirror, her hair dark too, falling to her shoulders. The man touched it with his fingertips, and Taylor thought that it looked very soft, could almost feel the texture in his imagination.

The young man sat back and signaled the bartender, but it was the boy who brought the menus, his father following with a glass of red wine for the young woman. Taylor could see her profile in the mirror as she clutched the man's wrist on the tabletop. She was lovely, as beautiful as the man was handsome. But her expression was distressed, her eyes welled with tears. Something had upset her, and the young man was trying to comfort, reaching to stroke her cheek.

Taylor saw that Ariel was watching them too, directly, not a reflection. The couple's pose reminded him of a scene from an old French film, black and white, the two of them as good looking as movie stars portraying a scene of grief and tenderness, the aftermath of something very sad. Triste.

He leaned over his own table and whispered to Ariel, "What do you think is wrong?"

She gave him a startled look.

"With the girl. Why is she so unhappy?"

"How would I know?"

"It can't be love. She has him, and he's obviously wild about her. Maybe it's grades. She did poorly on a test. Or didn't get a job she wanted."

The bartender's son brought their food, nervous for the plates in his hands, setting them down carefully. Ariel took a bite and chewed, so many times Taylor thought she would never swallow. Then she said, "Her parents. She's had a terrible argument with her parents."

Taylor wanted to say, who could argue with a girl like that, but instead asked, "Over what?"

Ariel shrugged. "They're jealous that she's so pretty."

"That would make them despicable people." Then it struck Taylor: The young woman was pregnant. She had just come from the doctor. Her parents would disown her. Her life had become a disaster.

The bartender put a plate of spaghetti in front of the young man. He twirled several strands on his fork and lifted it to the mouth of the young woman. Her food came a moment later, but Taylor couldn't watch any more, ashamed that he had seen so much. Why should people like that be unhappy, he wondered, aware that was the last thing he could say to Ariel. Father and daughter ate silently. When she said she didn't want another wine or dessert, he signaled for the check. They pushed back their chairs, his making a loud scraping noise. With a last glance, he saw the young man kiss the woman, just a brush of his lips on hers.

He was being foolish. No one suffered for getting pregnant these days. The young woman's woes were a mystery he would never solve.

"I know what it is," Ariel said, speaking low, barely moving her lips.

"What?"

"Someone died. Someone she loves died."

Out on the sidewalk, Taylor realized that he didn't know how to get back to the hotel, which way to turn. He was disoriented. Jet lag. Even the one beer. He could sense that Ariel was impatient, so he picked left, looking behind him at the dark looming shape of the building across the boulevard. Nothing looked familiar. But it was night, and he couldn't see clearly, the headlights of cars dazzling his vision.

After several blocks, they came to a wide avenue with trees along the sidewalk and an island in the middle, a long row of cars jammed at the intersection. Taylor waited for the traffic light, ready to cross to the other side, when he realized the street was blocked off by police wagons, policemen with weapons in their hands gesturing that drivers couldn't get through.

"Do you know where we are?" Ariel asked.

"I'm afraid not."

"Please find out. I'm exhausted."

Taylor stepped under a streetlamp to unfold his map and saw that they were on Boulevard de Port Royal and would have to maneuver through a tangle of streets to get to Rue Monge. "We'll have to backtrack, I'm afraid." He turned left and then at the next corner left again into a narrow row of shuttered shops and offices, no lights on the upper levels.

But midway a little old lady with a red hat emerged from shadows. Taylor noticed something in her gloved hand, realized it was a leash, a small round black and white dog waddling at her feet in the gutter. Ariel immediately knelt beside the animal, murmuring soft sounds, stroking the dog's head. The depth of her need made Taylor catch his breath. He had to look away.

He forced himself to speak to the old woman. "Bon chien," he said, and the woman knew immediately that he was not French. "Dix y neuf," she told him, pointing at the animal, holding up all ten fingers and again with just nine. "That's amazing," he spoke in English. "Fantastique." The woman nodded and moved on with her dog.

"Can you believe that?" Taylor said to Ariel. "Nineteen and still going for walks."

She was still kneeling. "The poor thing is desperate to live."

They walked silently for several more blocks, Taylor stopping several times to consult his map. Where Rue Saint Jacques crossed Rue Guy Lussac, Ariel suddenly stopped and sat on a bench. "I can't go on much longer."

He looked up and down for a taxi, knowing it was a wasted hope. He hadn't seen a taxi since they left Boulevard de Port Royal, and only a few there, locked in the traffic. "Why don't you rest for a while?

Taylor felt turned around, unsure what to do next. When he spread his map, he couldn't focus, couldn't locate the street. He had taken them too far, too soon. He had gotten them lost.

The street was quiet, no people out and only occasional cars passing by. Taylor took deep breaths, his back aching, his calf muscles knotted. It was stopping that did it. Standing still. He would be in pain all the way to the hotel. Once he found a way.

Then he heard sirens in the distance, the sound getting louder, and moments later a group of large young men running up the middle of the street toward them, five or six, two tripping over the jutting cobblestones and coming down hard on their hands and knees. They cursed and got up immediately, running again. Not far behind, three policemen were rushing after them, and approaching rapidly, a vehicle with a flashing blue light and a blaring noise.

As the men came close, Ariel stood from the bench and screamed. Don't, Taylor, thought; don't draw their attention. But she was screaming and trembling, and he clutched her just as her legs gave way. She fell against him, so heavy for a woman so thin, dead weight. He squeezed her tight, murmuring, "It will be all right. It will be all right. They don't care about us." They don't even see us, he thought; we're not part of this place.

One of the policemen stopped and lifted his weapon, but when the vehicle sped past him, let it fall to his side. Then they were all on the next block, the young men scattering into alleys and doorways, more policemen scrambling from the back of the vehicle.

Ariel stopped screaming, just stood and sobbed, still wrapped in her father's arms. Taylor couldn't remember the last time he had held her like this, so close to the pulse of her life. "They're gone now. It's OK." He wished he could tell her he loved her, could make himself say the words. He touched her hair and found it stiff, fixed with a spray.

Soon, he knew, she would stop and wipe her eyes, pull away from him as if nothing had happened. He would look at his map and, this time, trace a route. They would walk the final blocks back to the hotel, say goodnight and lie in their beds unable to sleep, waiting for the morning when they would begin their itinerary. For the next few days they would gaze at great art, eat fine food, marvel at the sweep of buildings that lined the Seine. They would stay far from protests and police and rioters and speak of nothing but beauty for the rest of their time in Paris.

RESTORING THE CASTLE

BRET LOVED THE STONES. Jagged blocks heaped against the hillside in a tangle of vines, tumbled onto what had been an inner courtyard. He would walk among them, rubbing calloused hands over their rough grey surfaces. Then he would close his eyes and imagine the castle whole again, walls standing, outlined against the clouds, a tower visible from the broad plain below.

The structure had been abandoned for hundreds of years, no more than a destination for climbers. Some had carved names and dates from centuries past into the stone, markings that charmed Bret, even though he hated the graffiti that marred modern cities. He would run a finger into the grooves of the letters, sensing a connection with long-dead men and women who had struggled up a rocky hillside to reach this place.

Bret was there with Marcič and his men to restore the castle, amid a clutter of steel scaffolds, block and tackle, wooden frames, buckets of viscous mortar. Marcič, an engineer, a native of the country, had official responsibility. Bret served as an advisor, the only foreigner in the group, paid by the international agency financing the project. From the very first day, Marcič had shrugged at Bret's eagerness and called what they were doing just a job, a way to keep his workers busy.

Bret couldn't understand. This castle belonged to his homeland's past. He reminded Marcič of its history.

Marcič shook his head. "That was all many centuries ago. It has nothing to do with who we are now. What we need now."

"But it's wonderful," Bret said, reaching out to brace himself against a fragment of wall. "Even as a ruin it's wonderful. Think of how beautiful it will be when we finish."

"Castles were cold, dank places. Always dark with those slits for windows. Always a stink from rotting food and human filth. Would you really want to live there and not in our trailers?"

"I'd like to try," Bret told him.

The four gleaming metal trailers sat side by side beneath trees outside what remained of the castle walls. The constant putter of their generators merged with the day's sounds—the bird songs, the waterfall, the wind through the leaves.

"It's spectacular here," Bret couldn't help repeating whenever he and Marcič had another of their consultations. "Up so high. Above everything." From the hilltop Bret could see the roofs of the scattered villages, the patterns of the fields, shining ponds, out as far as the wide river that was a border to another place.

And Marcič would answer, indicating his men with the sweep of a hand and then pointing down at a scene blurred by haze. "That's where we live. There's nothing for us up here. In our country a man is lucky to have work."

Bret knew this country was poor, its cities shabby, its people worn. But only once had he tried to argue that history mattered, that a country needed monuments to its past.

"Some would say," Marcič had told him, "all this is waste. The money should go to the people. The sick and the hungry."

"Are you one who would say that?" Bret asked.

"Not when the money is keeping me busy."

Bret smiled, but Marcič's lips were tight.

Even when it was whole, this castle had been a rough structure, a fortress for warlords, not a dwelling for nobles. Bret had helped restore those too, many roomed buildings of richly decorated walls, tiled floors, designs of Renaissance splendor. But those were in countries with centuries of wealth. Here people had always struggled, the castles fortresses for survival, not display. This one, when Bret first saw it, had been little more than a ruin, half the walls so deteriorated they seemed beyond rebuilding. The men spent weeks just cutting away the growth that clung to the surfaces.

To guide his planning, Bret had been supplied with a portfolio of information, faded daguerreotype photographs taken when the tall tower was still standing, copies of old sketches, a print of a painting from the early 1600s by the country's most famous artist, a man Bret had never heard of until he began to study the region's past. For weeks he had read little but books about the period when the castle was whole. Whenever he worked on a restoration, he tried to immerse himself in another age and shut out the effects of the present.

Most days, as much as he brooded over their exchanges, he and Marčič spoke only brief words about the immediate task, the two of them extending a tape measure or standing over one of Bret's diagrams spread on the base of a broken wall. Much of the time they helped the men move the stones, the largest clusters wrapped in chains, hoisted into the air on a hook from a rusted machine, the engine straining with sputter. Grunting and cursing, they guided the stones into place, great weights even for a group of men. Slick with sweat, they took long rests and swigged from canteens whenever a cluster was replaced.

Other times they would gather the stones scattered across the ground, forming a human link to pass them up the embankments, one after another, laying them on a base and fixing their position with a rough mortar that they smeared with bare hands. When their flesh began to shrivel and sting, they would drip their hands into a bucket of rainwater and rub them with a filthy towel.

The process exhilarated Bret, the physical effort, the satisfaction of each step that brought the actual castle closer to the one that lived in his imagination. He would have liked to shout, chant songs as he had on other projects. Yet he knew to swallow his excitement and stay silent. These men hated what they had to do, felt themselves reduced to beasts of burden. Marčič didn't have to tell him that. Bret knew from their faces. Marčič was the only one who spoke English, his status complex. He had to demonstrate that he understood Bret's planning while asserting his authority. If he spent too much time with Bret, shut the others out of their English conversations, they would resent him. Bret kept his frustration to himself. On other projects there had been people to talk with, sharing the dedication.

Down in one of the village markets, he probably would not be able to distinguish Marčič and his workers in the crowd, all the men of the region short and stubby, with flat tanned faces and narrow eyes, heads of thick dark curls, muscled arms, and hard round bellies protruding over their belts. Here the workers wore mud-crusted jeans and torn tee shirts emblazoned with names of cities they would never see—Paris, Firenze, Londres, Vein. Each shirt keyed a vivid memory for Bret, deep pleasures of food, wine, art, architecture. When he first saw the shirts, Bret's impulse was to smile, but he knew enough to turn away and set his face.

At the end of the long workday, the sky light till past ten, Marčič and the men would sprawl on the grass by the trailer, backs against tree

trunks, and drank the local wine, bitter and pale. Bret sat away from
them, watching the night swallow the castle until it was only a dark shape
in the moonlight.

The voices of the men, the harsh, abrupt sounds of their language, were
lost to him, obliterated by the rhythms of the generators. He wondered if
they kept their speech low because he was near, even though they knew he
could not decipher their words. Did they have secrets from him? They never
laughed. They never revealed pleasure or disagreement. He could not imagine what they had to say to each other but would not think of asking Marcič. They sat like that for hours, long past midnight, as if fulfilling a ritual.

Though the men were not far from their homes on the plain, no more
than an hour on foot, they never went down to visit their families. For
Bret, it was almost as if they saw themselves in two distinct worlds—the
castle and the flatland—that could never mix.

Bret came to wonder about the myths of the country, whether after so
many centuries these men, descendants of peasants, still lived with a vesti-
gial fear of the castle, of the warlords who had subjugated their ancestors.

And that made him think about his own situation, his freedom to
move around the world, finding himself at home wherever he went, even
when—as in most cases—he didn't know the language. The buildings, the
architecture, the scenery moved him. It excited him to be in the midst of
centuries, the palpable presence of the past.

It wasn't that he was wealthy. He had no permanent job, no savings
to speak of. Instead, he went from grant to grant, project to project, confi-
dent that something new would materialize soon after the last one ended.
The agencies respected his abilities; they sought him out. And he considered himself young, healthy, and vigorous, many years ahead before he
would have to worry about the future.

When it began to rain, not heavily, just enough to make the stones
too slippery to handle, Bret suggested to Marcič that they give the men a
break. The thick dark clouds promised to linger for several more days, and
they just waited in their trailers. "They might as well go home and spent
some time in their villages. You too."

"They won't go," Marcič told him.

"But they haven't seen their families in weeks."

"Their families are somewhere else."

"I don't understand. Where?"

"Where it's safe."

Bret stepped out from their shelter, the rain stinging his face, and tried to look down at the plain, seeing nothing but a thick fog. "This isn't a storm. The river won't flood. What are they worried about?"

Marcič grunted, shrugged, and turned his back.

In his trailer, one he had all to himself, his maps and papers arranged in neat racks, Bret turned on his shortwave radio and ran through the bands, trying to find news that would give him an explanation. Aside from snatches of music and a few fading voices in strange languages, he received only a static hiss, no matter how he angled the antenna or turned the small receiver. He knew almost nothing of this country's present beyond its poverty and reports of occasional unrest, farmers protesting outside government buildings. He had come to this site almost directly from the airport, half dozing from the flight until he arrived.

For the next two days, protected by a Gore-Tex poncho, Bret measured stones and painted small numbers on their sides, the likely order of an original arrangement, pieces of a puzzle. He heard nothing from the trailers, not even signs of cooking. The men ate cold food and opened their doors only to dispose of the tins.

Then the rain stopped suddenly, and a warm afternoon sun burned through the haze, the damp ground steaming in the heat. Marcič gave a command, and the men appeared, returning to their work as if they had never stopped. Bret nodded to them, gave them small smiles, but they looked away and did not respond.

When the fog below lifted, he moved off from the castle, out on a path to a ridge, and peered at the plain with his binoculars. He had packed them for birds and flowers, to magnify nature. Now he scanned the villages for clues about the families. Some were too far off for him to see anything but the patchwork of red rooftops. Here and there, a truck or a tractor moved out in the fields, but rarely on the streets. He found few signs of people. But in one of the towns with a large central square, black military vehicles stood circled around a fountain—tanks and trucks, artillery caissons, even a bulldozer. Bret thought he saw men in uniforms sitting on a brick wall and twisted the focus knob for clarity, but the lenses weren't powerful enough.

He hurried back to the castle to confront Marcič. "What's happening down there?"

"I don't know."

"You knew enough to send your families away."

"Perhaps it will be nothing. You can never be sure."

The men had stopped working to stare at Marcič, a huge stone swaying over their heads.

"If it is something," Bret insisted, "what will it be?"

"Nobody likes the government."

"Why not?"

"They are other people."

"What other people?"

"Invaders. People who lived in this castle."

"That was centuries ago." Bret shook his head in frustration. The information had been in the documents, so insignificant to him that he had just skimmed. Barons, no more than tribal chieftains, had taken the religion of past conquerors and dominated the region. "Ancient history."

"Nothing is ancient here."

Bret pointed down at the town. "Whose tanks are those?"

"Ours."

Bret saw the satisfaction in Marcič's eyes.

"Will there be revolution? Fighting?"

The men seemed to understand those words. Bret saw it on their faces. Marcič shouted at them, the first time he had raised his voice in all their weeks together, and they began placing the stones again.

"How bad will it be, Marcič?" Bret found himself angry—at Marcič, at the workers, at the men in uniform, and the whole country. It was so stupid, such a waste. They would kill, maim, destroy, and end up worse off no matter who was in charge.

From the set of his mouth, Marcič was angry too. "You don't live here. It's none of your business."

"What about the castle?"

"Why should we care about this place?"

"Will you keep working?"

Marcič turned away and went to the men, huddled in a group, whispering beside the stone.

In the evening, while the men were eating, Marcič gestured to Bret to come to him inside one of the castle walls. Bret hoped the man would apologize. He was ready to reach out and shake hands, say that he was sorry himself. But Marcič was standing in a corner, looking down at the

floor, kicking at a pile of rubble.

"Come see what the men found," he said.

Bret followed his gaze and saw a pocked grating of rusted iron, and below a small cylindrical chamber, lined with moss-covered brick, barely a meter across. He knew immediately what it was, yet let Marcič explain.

"A dungeon. A torture chamber. They put men down there. People like me. They didn't have room to sit. They stood until they starved."

Marcič was smiling at him, but there was no pleasure in his expression.

"Is that worse," Bret asked him—imagining prisoners flailing at the brick, screaming, clawing with bloody fingers—"than what people do to each other now?"

"The same thing," Marcič said. "Always with people it's the same thing." He gestured out at the castle, and Bret saw that most of it was still a ruin.

"It's ugly here." Marcič pointed down at the plain. "It's ugly every-where."

Bret shook his head. "That's your country. I've been where it's beau-tiful. So many places."

"No! You don't see what's real. Wherever you've been, it was ugly there before. It will be again."

The next morning, Bret heard the first sounds of gunfire, muffled by distance, one isolated boom and then a steady fusillade. He expected the men to panic, stop their work and rush for a view of the plain. Instead, they kept frozen faces and passed stones from hand to hand. Bret was the one who could not resist looking. He stood out on a broken parapet and stared into his binoculars, turning left and right. At first, he saw nothing, then puffs of smoke and, after another barrage, the bright dance of flames. Moments later, there was more smoke, more fire, and he could no longer watch.

Back with the workers, Bret offered the glasses to Marcič, without a word, just extending an arm. Marcič spat into the dust and leaned his weight into the stone.

Then the sounds stopped. Perhaps, Bret wondered, it had been a short battle, a quick surrender. There would be a new government. They would bury the dead. Nothing would change. But an airplane passed overhead, startling them all with a harsh roar, trailing white vapor. And he knew it wasn't over. This time, the explosion was loud, nearby, sending a shudder through the hillside.

"They won't come here?" he said to Marcič, more a question that a statement. "Why should they come here? What's here?"

"They hate this place. My people have always hated this place."

"Let's stop everything else and concentrate on the tower. No matter what happens, let's rebuild the tower."

Marcič gave an abrupt nod as if it didn't matter to him what they did. Bret kept them working long past their normal quitting time, signaling instructions, no longer bothering to go through Marcič, no longer caring about the man's status, his dignity, and Marcič said nothing, not to him.

Bret neglected his careful measuring. There wasn't time to make sure the right stones went back in place, that the fit was exact. He just wanted to see the tower restored as quickly as possible, the structure reaching upward, seen for miles, above the fighting.

He worked with the men, all of them shirtless in the heat, erecting scaffolding, wood planks on a metal frame, lifting stones over their heads, one after another, barely stopping to eat, just chewing at tough processed meat, washing it down with swigs of wine. Bret found himself covered with scratches, thin scabs crusting across his arms and his chest. The men were cut too, smears of their blood on the stones.

The noises of war—the explosions, the tank rounds, the occasional bomb—became just more sounds of the day, with the bird calls and the wind and the generators. Bret didn't bother to look any more, ignoring the fires below.

In early evening, Marcič shouted at the men, a short explosion of words, more excited than Bret had ever seen him. The men climbed down from the scaffolding and walked to their trailers. "What? What it is?" he demanded. But Marcič ignored him and closed his door. When he and the men emerged, they were dressed in black, faces smeared with soot, the bulge of weapons under their shirts.

Bret could not breathe, chill, shivering, certain they would turn and shoot him, round after round, a fury of revenge. Instead, they lined up and walked back into the trees, Marcič their leader.

Bret stood frozen until they had disappeared. He picked up a stone and set it atop a wall, another, then gave up, knowing it was a futile.   A rumbling shook the earth beneath his feet, much louder than all the other sounds. Looking down through the twist of branches, he saw the tank at the bottom of the hillside, its angle steep, pushing upward, crushing the underbrush, uprooting trees, its gun turret swaying left and right. Nothing would stop it.

Within an hour there would be no castle, not even a ruin, just shattered rubble beyond restoration. Far below, on the plain, people would rejoice.

AWFUL ADVICE

RICHARD STILL COULDN'T KEEP HIS HANDS OFF DOLORES after six months of eager caresses, even here in the waiting lounge at JFK Gate 37. Though they were in early middle age, parents of five between them, he clung to her as if touch were an addiction. Richard saw that strangers were embarrassed by his public desire. But he couldn't stop, didn't care. He pressed his mouth to the nape of her neck. "You're my queen and my empress," he whispered. "I'm going to honor you every night in London." When her fingers stroked his knee, he swallowed and closed his eyes.

"I see you've got a Nicholson's guide." Richard sensed a looming presence and looked up.

There stood a large, flushed man with a midsection that overflowed stiff new jeans. A nest of slicked grey hair gleamed beneath the ceiling lights as he fixed them with a hooded stare.

"We also use Nicholson's *London*." The voice resounded from a nose that sprawled across the face like a mountain range.

Richard glanced down at the red paperback protruding from the man's carry-on. Dolores shifted away, slightly, leaving just a brush of contact.

"The travel agent recommended it," Richard said, trying to push his own copy deeper into a pocket.

"It's very useful." The man stepped closer, blocking the light. "It lists everything. Museums. Wine bars. Vegetarian restaurants. All night chemists. Shops where you can buy bespoke hats and family crests and custom-made umbrellas with secret swords. We have four copies. One for each of us."

He gestured toward the plastic bench across the aisle, at a heavy bosomed woman who appeared to be upholstered in tapestry, her mouth twisted as if she had just bitten into something rotten. Beside her sat two young women of about twenty in ballerina slippers and pink gossamer dresses, one with loose wispy hair a shade lighter than that piled atop her sister's head. Both gazed out like sleepwalkers.

"I'm sure the book will be useful," Richard said.

"You'll probably find yourselves overwhelmed." The man leaned toward them and pointed a finger. "We visit London every summer. Don't be ashamed to ask for my help."

When he turned and strode away, Richard pulled Dolores close again and rolled his eyes. "What an awful man," she murmured, exciting him with the soft hum of her voice. "An awful family," he echoed.

•

In the plane while Dolores dozed with her head vibrating against his chest, Richard couldn't sleep, snapping awake at each bounce of an air pocket and forever opening his eyes to one of the Awfuls—a daughter floating down the aisle toward the toilets, Mrs. rattling seatbacks as she reached up to the overhead compartment for another sweater, Mr. Awful tapping shoulders to find someone who would listen to his analysis of the in-flight movie.

•

"Look!" Richard called. Dolores blinked and shielded her eyes from the glare of sunrise.

He pointed down at the shaded squares of green beneath them, here and there a glittering pond, the silver twisting of a river. "It's England!" He watched her face glow.

"Oh my God!" She squeezed his hand in both of hers. "It really is."

"A whole new country just for us."

"It's my dream."

He turned into her view and suddenly kissed her. Her mouth froze in surprise, then opened warmly.

She was even lovelier than the woman he had imagined in his years of midnight longings, since the summer day she appeared on his street, stepping long legs from a mud-splattered station wagon. And she had sensed his yearning for her all the time they were behaving like nothing more than neighbors, crying out in the moonlight, half laughing, half sobbing, when he finally took her in his arms.

She drew back from his kiss, smiling as she pushed him aside. "Let me look. I want to see everything." She gave a gasp of delight when the plane banked and revealed a vivid greenness spreading to the horizon. "You don't know how I longed for this moment. All those years with Ernie."

"I'd hardly have known England existed," he told her, "if it wasn't for you."

"If Ernie were beside me now, he'd only care about finding something down there to shoot."

Richard thought she was joking until he saw her tears. "Oh, love!" His heart swelled.

"My whole life I wanted beauty," she whispered, "and I spent fifteen years with a man who lined our walls with weapons."

Tears streamed down his face. "We'll love each other even more in London."

"It will be wonderful in London," she insisted.

•

Richard knew this trip was a risk, potential ammunition against them in divorce court. There would be custody battles when they got back home. Now Virginia wouldn't let him see the boys, dragged them to her mother every weekend, and Ernie called twice a week to curse Dolores as an unfit parent. But they had been desperate to get away from small-town scandal— the ringing phones, the stares in the supermarket, the sullen looks of his sons when they passed on the street, the betrayal on the faces of her children.

•

After they landed at Gatwick, jet-lagged, shuffling after the other passengers through a maze of ramps, stairways, and corridors, they watched Mr. Awful lead his family into the wrong line at Passport Control, waving his arms high above his head and calling "Follow me, follow me" into the cluster of British nationals. When a woman in a uniform blocked his path, he shouted, "It wasn't this way last year," and pushed his wife and daughters into the midst of the foreigners, just ahead of Richard and Dolores.

In the baggage area, while Dolores stood guard over the suitcase already retrieved from the carousel, Richard saw the sisters wrestling a luggage cart from a bearded man and Mr. Awful striding among the travelers dispensing advice on how to stack, pack, and carry. He lifted the nametag from Dolores' case and told her, "Never put down your home address. Thieves work in airports to find out who's left unguarded houses behind."

Most of the people from the plane headed for the express train to London, but Mr. Awful directed his family toward the taxis. "We've got too much planned to waste time here." His declaration rang out over the din in the terminal.

"Thank goodness they're gone," Dolores sighed.

Richard nodded agreement, breathing her perfume, nuzzling her earlobe.

•

Victoria Station was mobbed, the streets swarming, the taxi queue a hundred yards long. Richard's arms ached from the two heavy suitcases, but Dolores bubbled expectation. When a cab finally drove them off, she sat forward, pointing out glimpses of what seemed to be palaces and cathedrals as they twisted in and out a tangle of streets, through parks, around circuses.

For Richard everything seemed to be happening in fast forward—the flash of red buses, the figures scurrying on the sidewalks, the grey blur of buildings. He had expected grandeur and openness, not the sensation of being trapped inside a maze.

But Dolores's face was radiant. Richard turned from the city to lose himself in her fascination, following each of her gestures, every nuance of her expression, with a thrill of rediscovery.

She shifted back and forth on the seat, turning from window to window, laughing at her own frustration. "There's so much. I can't get a clear look at anything."

•

Throughout the long famine of marriage to Ernie, London had become the magic city of Dolores' dreams, kept vivid by glossy picture books she spread across Richard's lap as they planned their trip, pointing out domes, arches, gardens, and spires. "It's hard to believe," she would say, looking up from the book toward the bland streets outside her window, "that so much splendor really exists in the world."

If the choice had been his, Richard would have picked an island lush with dazzling colors, the two of them in a private paradise, making love beneath a brilliant sun on soft white sands. But eager to please her, he had cashed in an IRA despite the teller's warning that he would have to pay a penalty.

•

Their hotel, the Wellingham, that had appeared so elegant in the travel agent's brochure turned out to have minuscule rooms and no closet, just a hulking dark wardrobe whose door kept swinging open and two narrow single beds with crudely patched brown spreads.

"Do we have to stay here?" Dolores asked him.

"We've paid in advance," Richard said.

"But I wanted everything to be . . . beautiful."

When he thought she might cry, he whispered consolingly that she was tired, that everything would look better once she'd rested.

Richard beckoned her to his bed. Dolores insisted they stretch out for only a few minutes, keep themselves awake despite the jet lag and begin exploring right away. "I don't want to waste a second."

"Yes, yes," he said as he slid in beside her and led her into a lingering lovemaking. They slept deeply until late afternoon. Voices in the hallway woke them, Richard's arm stiff from the weight of her shoulder on the cramped mattress.

•

Dolores wanted tea. "Tea in London." She laughed as if the idea were beyond belief. Richard asked at the desk and was pointed toward the hotel's coffee shop down a corridor where floorboards creaked under threadbare carpeting.

The waitress brought two tepid pots and a plate of dry scones surrounded by little tins of jam. Richard, suddenly famished, spread a cherry paste on a scone that broke in his hand. He swallowed it in two sweet bites and licked the crumbs from his fingertips.

Dolores just sipped and nibbled. "Are you ok?" he asked.

"I'm fine."

"I don't want you to be disappointed."

She smiled and touched his hand. "We're going to see London the right way. All we have to do is know where we're looking, and we'll discover wonders around every corner." She slipped a hand inside his jacket and pulled out the Nicholson's. "We'll be guided by the experts."

•

For Richard, Buckingham Palace turned out to be a dull block of a building behind an acre of gravel, the guards ridiculous under the black puffs on their heads. Dolores stretched to tiptoe, trying to look over the people who blocked her view. When she braced a hand on his shoulder to raise herself up, he wrapped arms around her and lifted her into the air.

"Oh!" She cried out in surprise. "What did you see?"

"Their uniforms are wonderful!"

"Are they what you expected?"

"Oh yes. Marvelous!"

Behind them taxis and double-decker buses rumbled past on the broad roadway, filling his head with diesel fumes.

•

At street corners, bewildered by the "Look Left," "Look Right" warning stamped into the pavement, Richard clung to Dolores. Cars bore down from unexpected directions. "Be careful," he urged, afraid to trust his instincts.

Dolores laughed. "Haven't you noticed? The drivers stop for pedestrians. People here are very polite."

Everywhere they went Dolores held the Nicholson's guide open, referring to it whenever a new view appeared. After a stroll along the Mall, they stood overlooking Trafalgar Square at twilight, the National Gallery spread behind them, stone lions crouched beside the fountain, Nelson's Column towering above. Pigeons swooped and fluttered, pecking crumbs at their feet.

"Wouldn't it be wonderful if we never had to go home?" Dolores said. He touched fingertips to her hair.

"I've never felt so excited!" She reached open arms toward the city. "There's so much. I can't decide what to do next. Let's find Westminster Abbey."

"Head straight down Whitehall," a voice behind them announced. "But it closed two hours ago."

Before he turned, Richard guessed what he would find. Mr. Awful in a safari jacket, Mrs. rotund in Burberry plaid, one daughter in what seemed to be harem pants, the other in a dirndl.

"Where are you staying?" Mr. Awful said.

"The Wellingham." Richard answered reluctantly.

Mr. Awful shook his head. "You should have asked us. The Wellingham isn't what it used to be. The last time we stayed there my daughter found stains on her sheet." He didn't indicate which daughter. "We checked out in the morning."

"Where are you?" Dolores asked. "The Boughton."

"My husband is an expert on London hotels." Mrs. Awful said, conveying enthusiasm even though her face still seemed twisted into a wince.

"Have you chosen a restaurant for dinner?" Mr. Awful asked. "We haven't thought about it," Richard said.

The daughters stared up at the column. They had inherited their father's somnolent eyes and their mother's pinched mouth.

"The Stratton has an excellent carving table. We eat there on every visit."

"Why don't you join us?" Mrs. Awful said.

"That's very kind," Richard said, "but we have other plans."

Mr. Awful tapped his wife. "Can't you see that these people don't want to be bothered with a family. They want to eat by candlelight and gaze into each other's eyes."

Dolores slipped her hand from Richard's, but he seized it and squeezed.

•

Dolores, maps fixed in her memory, insisted that they walk everywhere to really know the city, miles and miles each day: down Drury Lane to the Strand, beside the Embankment, across Westminster Bridge, along the

South Bank, back over to Charing Cross, from the Marble Arch to Brompton Road. And everywhere Dolores recognized sights from her picture books. Some nights, she fell exhausted onto her bed, kicking off shoes, heaping clothing on the rug, within minutes deep in a heavy sleep.

Richard would prop himself up to watch her face in the moonlight that filtered through the drapes. It was a lovely face, the features finely formed, the brown hair soft around it. He longed to hold it in his hands, feel the shape of her lips.

In the morning, no matter how early Richard awoke, Dolores was already dressed, leafing through the guide, planning their itinerary, writing down lists, even calculating distances on the scale of miles.

But as much as they saw, as much as they did, Richard couldn't wait for the day to end so that he could draw her down beside him.

•

Wherever they went, there were always crowds—clustered around the Ming vases in the British Museum, pressing to glimpse the jewels in the Tower, queuing for half-price theater tickets in Leicester Square, pawing through cashmere sweaters on Regent Street, sampling cheeses in Harrods' food halls.

Dolores bought a paisley-covered journal to note all that they saw, all that they did, on cool ivory pages.

•

Except for a brief sunset one evening, it had been grey through the days, the occasional drizzles so faint they hardly felt them. But one afternoon as they shopped along Oxford Street, a sudden rain pelted down, sharp and chill. All around them people popped open black umbrellas. Richard darted into a doorway, expecting Dolores to follow behind him. But she was standing in the middle of the sidewalk, arms spread, face turned upward into the stream of water.

•

As they crossed a cobblestone courtyard outside a tiny twelfth-century church, a carriage clattered through an entrance gate, drawn by four black horses in gleaming harnesses.

Dolores clutched Richard's arm. "I can't believe it."

A groom in livery leaped down to open the carriage door. Two men stepped out, wearing tails and stiff top hats, bright red flowers in their lapels. One was white-haired with a trim shaped beard, the other ruddy and mustached.

The bearded man reached inside the carriage and drew out a woman all in pink—pink dress, pink shoes and stockings, a pink hat with a brim that touched her shoulder. When she stepped to the cobblestone, a breeze caught the hat and she had to clutch it to her hair, throwing her head back

in laughter. The men laughed too.

Then another woman emerged, layered in white lace, long blonde hair under a veil, her throat wrapped in strands of pearls.

"How beautiful," Dolores said, face aglow, happier that Richard had ever seen her. "She's going to marry one of those men in that church. What a life she'll have!"

Richard surged with anger because these strangers were giving her such joy. "It's all an act," he said.

"What?"

"The fancy clothes, the horse and carriage, this old church. It's nothing but a costume party. They're trying to pretend this crumbling stinking place is beautiful."

•

In their room, as soon as the door clicked shut, Richard folded Dolores into his embrace, slid a hand under her sweater. But she didn't seem to notice, her eyes fixed in thought. She pulled free of him and drifted toward the window, brushing her cheek against an edge of the drapes and looking out over the traffic, listening to the groans of heavy engines.

"What's wrong?" he said.

"You're spoiling it, Richard."

"Me! What have I done?"

"It's the way you feel."

He looked at himself in the mirror, the back of her head reflected behind him, and knew he shouldn't speak. But he couldn't stop the words. "I'm so damn sick of the paintings and the porcelain, the gilded moldings and the inlaid tables. None of that stuff has anything to do with us. We don't need London."

•

They stumbled across the Awfuls in St. James Park, Mr. and Mrs. sprawled on canvas chairs alongside the pond, Mr. feeding crumbs to the herringbone ducks, Mrs. looking up at the domes of the government buildings.

"We have tickets for the opera for this evening," Mrs. Awful called before Richard could get away.

"We were there yesterday," Richard told her.

Mrs. Awful squinted up suspiciously and gestured toward the two girls batting a balloon back and forth on the other side of the pond. "My daughters saw you in Parliament Square."

"It must have been someone else," he insisted.

Mr. Awful showed an empty hand to the ducks. "You're both in the midst of a divorce, aren't you?"

"How did you know?" Richard stood rigid, gripping Dolores' wrist in a cold clutching.

"My husband is a student of human character," Mrs. Awful said.

Dolores smiled at the woman.

"Then he must know that I'm running away from home."

"May I give you some advice?" he said.

Dolores nodded, expectant, Richard pulling at her arm. "London isn't a city for passion."

Richard shuddered with an urge to tip over the man's chair and kick him into the pond. "You don't know anything!" he shouted. Then in the sudden silence he felt the eyes of the others on him, Dolores nodding along with the Awfuls even though none of them was moving a muscle. He stomped through a brilliant flower bed into thick green shrubs and hoped she would follow.

•

"I was twenty when I met Ernie," Dolores said. It was long past midnight and they lay on separate beds staring up into the darkness. "He kept telling me how wonderful I was, how much he loved me. I let myself believe I was a special person."

"You are special. You're perfect. It's him. He didn't realize how lucky he was."

She stayed silent for so long he thought she had forgotten his presence. Then she asked, "Didn't you love Virginia once?"

"I thought I did. I didn't know what love was until I met you."

"She has a sweet face. But she's thirty pounds overweight. The first time I saw her I thought, what a dumpy woman. I've stayed slim, Richard. Maybe what you really love is my waistline." She reached out to touch his arm.

He twisted away from her soothing. "It was a mistake to come here."

•

Richard closed his eyes while Dolores brushed her teeth. When she stepped out of the bathroom, he heard the creak of her mattress and then gazed over at the dark hump of her blanket.

Without a word he crawled in beside her and fixed her mouth with a kiss that drove her head into the pillow. He twisted her gown up above her waist and winced at the abrasive dryness, the whole time thinking, love me, love me.

He stayed beside her on the narrow bed all night, wondering if she were sleeping as little as he, but not daring to speak, afraid of what she might say. When daylight glowed around the edge of the drapes he tried to be tender, caressing her shoulders, brushing light kisses across her forehead, down her cheeks. She lay inert under his touch until he rolled away. Then she kicked her legs from under the blanket and stepped toward the bathroom.

"It's not just passion," he called to the closed door. "I need you." The shower blasted spray against the plastic curtain.

•

Their flight back home was very crowded. Richard heard someone say it was the time of year, the end of the vacation season. Although they arrived hours before departure time, they couldn't get a seat together.

Richard protested, raising his voice to make the clerk understand how vital it was that they return home side by side. But the clerk, a freckled woman with a clipped accent, stayed cool. The computer offered no options; perhaps they could make an exchange on the plane. Dolores told her it was all right.

Their rows, five apart, got the first call to board. They merged into the line still deciding who would carry which hand baggage. He ended up with the presents for his sons, she with those for her children. They would sort out the others after landing.

On the plane, Richard turned, trying for glimpses of her, but the seat-back blocked his view. Dolores had a window, squeezed in beside two shapeless women with blonde-dyed curls who cradled duty free bags on their laps and argued about which stores they had purchased their sweaters in.

Richard sat in the middle seat. At the window a boy in shiny black shirt and trousers was already plugged into earphones, jerking his shoulders to a rhythm Richard could not hear. He peered over the boy to watch the ground crew, men in orange coveralls making last minute checks of the wing flaps. Richard tried to imagine how it would feel to crash, whether he would experience a terrible pain or just lose consciousness.

The aisle seat beside him thumped heavily. But Richard would not turn his head.

"Tell me where you've been since we met in the park," the man said. "What you saw."

Without looking at him, Richard recited lists, speaking through the taxiing and the takeoff, the force of climbing that pained his ears, repeating Dolores' itineraries. In his mind the sound of her voice echoed like a distant memory.

"But you've missed so much," Mr. Awful said.

Richard's eyes flooded. "I didn't know where to look."

"You should have asked me. I know what's important."

CANALS

ON HIS FIRST FULL DAY IN LEIDEN, though bleary with jetlag, despite the humid heat, Russell stuck to his plan to explore the canals, dragging himself from the strange bed and renting a kayak at the Beestenmarkt quay. He had studied a tourist's map of the city for weeks before his arrival, fascinated by the pattern of blue waterways that intersected the streets, envisioning sailboats gliding across a brilliant surface. But there, legs extended in a yellow shell, paddling with muscles that ached after the first strokes, he realized how wrong he had been. Few people actually used the canals. A half-empty tour launch churned across his path, and now and then a houseboat bobbed at the seawall.

Despite the pain, his arms found a smooth rhythm, a steady splash of dipping blades, a fine spray in his face. Above him, at odd angles, he saw the tile roofs of houses, upper windows shimmering in the sun, treetops, church spires, slender willow branches billowing over an embankment, the gleaming metal of parked cars, rows of chained bicycles, striped canvas stalls of a street market, people at the edge oblivious to his presence. He passed under bridges, suddenly cool beneath a canopy of damp brick, swallowed by shadows, then shooting out into the light.

Russell heaved forward, sweat streaming, his shirt saturated. He unbuttoned the front, hesitant to take it off because of the blazing sun. When he looked up into the brightness, his head spun and he forced back a spasm of nausea. It was a mistake to be out here on such a day.

Russell realized he was lost, the map in his belly pack useless. The more he paddled, the more he felt he was fighting a current that would sweep him out to an endless sea. Exhausted, he cradled the paddle in his arms and let himself drift. In a moment of dizziness, he felt a sensation of the kayak flipping, his head plunged into murky water, staring down at a grotesque realm.

His eyes stung with tears, burning from his own body salt, as if he had failed a test, his first effort in a new country. Then he told himself he was being ridiculous, stupid for not sleeping till noon, for rushing things. He had to take time, move step by step and not give Janice the satisfaction of his defeat.

He knew what he must do: he wiped his face with his shirttail, tied the kayak to an embankment, climbed up to the street, and sat on a bench with eyes closed, heart racing, the soft splash of water below.

•

After a fitful sleep, Russell stood by a window of his apartment looking beyond the courtyard below, out past the wrought iron fence at the canal to the rear of his building. The rental had been arranged over the Internet, a temporary accommodation while he explored. Yet it amazed him to think that he was actually here, in the Netherlands, gazing at this scene. He had been watching for an hour, but very little was happening. The opaque water seemed absolutely still. On the other side men and women rode bicycles along the narrow street, a few walking; here and there a door opened and someone stepped out onto the sidewalk. It struck him how little he knew about this city, who these people were and what they did.

Two cats, one black and white and the other grey, sprang onto the courtyard from a ground floor apartment, arching their backs and then curling in plastic chairs. Russell called to them with sharp hissing sounds but neither looked up. Once again, he missed the pets he had to leave behind. Someday soon, he told himself, he would learn these cats' names and stroke their warm fur.

The quiet of the day, the sleep of the animals, was making him drowsy, about to drop onto the sofa and close his eyes, wondering if only a fool would relocate his life so totally. Then the black double doors of the structure at the rear of the courtyard flung open, and a young blonde woman ran barefoot across the bricks, disappearing into the back entrance of his building. Her footsteps slapped on the stairway, and in seconds she was pounding at his door, rattling the knob.

Russell opened it quickly and looked into pale, terrified eyes. "A rat!" she cried.

He rushed after her down into the courtyard. The black and white cat lifted its head to glance at them and yawned. Russell followed her into what he had thought was a garage but now realized was her living quarters—a mattress tipped against one wall, a table and two wooden chairs on a bright scatter rug, a TV set with wide rabbit ears, clothes hanging from a metal bar. Fine dust swirled in the shaft of light that streamed through a single window high in the wall.

"Where?" he said, scanning the room, expecting a scurry of dull fur.

She pointed to the mattress, and he pulled it away from the wall to startle the creature, unsure what he would do when he exposed it. But there was nothing, only the baseboard. He searched behind the furniture, inside a cardboard box, under a pile of clothes, while the young woman stood in the center of the room digging toes into the rug.

"It probably ran out when you did," he told her, "as frightened of you as you were of it. Do you get rats often?"

"No, that was the first." She shivered and pulled the front of her garment tighter. Russell realized she was wearing a shiny pink robe, not a dress. At first glance with her short blonde hair and light blue eyes, he had taken her for very young, no more than twenty. But now, standing beside her, he saw that she was past thirty, perhaps even older, a big woman, as tall as he was.

It struck Russell that they were speaking English and wondered if he were so obviously American, but decided not to ask, as if that question would reveal how raw he was.

She shook her head, fluffing the layers of her hair, smoothing it back with her fingers, lifting her arms and stretching. Russell had the sense that these gestures were a performance. Then she reached out to shake his hand. "You can call me Tat."

"Is that a Dutch name?"

"It's a name." She smiled for the first time, lips thin and teeth uneven. Russell introduced himself.

"You're new," she said. "You just arrived."

"Yesterday. How did you know to come for me?"

"You were standing at the window."

Russell tried to place her accent. Her English was easy, but the pronunciation kept shifting, as if she had learned the language in several different countries. "Are you from Leiden?" he asked.

"Now I am." She crossed the room and knelt to open the small refrigerator, the robe flapping back from her knees. "Would you like a beer?"

Russell looked down and realized she had painted each of her toenails a different shade of red. Then he saw how dirty her feet were and felt a clutch in his middle. If he stayed one more minute, he would be over-powered by a need to wash them clean. "Another time," he said, backing away, unable to look at her.

"Yes, perhaps some other time." She sat on the rug, legs folded beneath her, and lifted a bottle to her lips. After a long draught, she wiped foam from her chin.

When he stepped into the courtyard, she did not close her doors. As he passed the grey cat, Russell reached to stroke fingertips across its back, sure Tat was watching him from the shadows of her room.

•

Russell had chosen Leiden from a guidebook, an ideal location to prepare for a new life devoted to flowers, the city only minutes from the bulb fields of Keukenhof and the great auction hall at Aalsmeer. For a decade, tulips had been his hobby, his fantasy—the delight of buds, the vibrancy of colors, the wonder of shapes. At home, he would spend evening hours and Sundays in his small greenhouse at the corner of the yard, out digging in the soft earth after the first thaw.

Janice rented videos, almost every night, and watched by herself. They had married too young and soon realized they had little to share. When the children still lived home, Russell assumed he and Janice would endure the rest of their lives in silent indifference, she strewing a mess behind her—dishes in the sink, clothes on the floor, he constantly picking up and putting away, long past the point of annoyance. It was just something he did because he needed order. But, just months after his younger son left, his marriage of almost thirty years reached a fierce end unimaginable at its beginning.

One evening Russell found Janice sprawled on the bed, face in a pillow, body shaking with sobs. He stood over her, hand poised, but could not make himself reach out. "What's wrong?" he had asked. "Everything," she moaned. "It's all been such a waste." "Me too," he told her, not certain whether she heard, then walked out and closed the door. Within days, there were vicious confrontations that left them both trembling with rage, his wife screaming, "I don't want you in my life!"

Desperate to escape, he abandoned the house to her, the cars, gave her custody of the cats. His children were adults, settled so far away he rarely saw them. He could get by for quite a while on his half of the profit from selling his trophy shop. It had always seemed so foolish, people spending money to glorify such trivial accomplishments. Now, for the first time he could recall, he had obligations to no one, and he craved another existence in a place totally new, free from the complications of memories. He would learn the secrets of flowers and become a man restored.

•

His daughter Marci had teased him about his going in their final phone conversation the week before he left. She lived two thousand miles away, and he hadn't seen her in three years, since the day of her wedding to a man from her company's home office. "She hates what you're doing," Janice had insisted, as if the divorce were his choice, his fault. But Russell didn't believe her. Unlike her sister and brother, Marci had been pleasant to him, never once alluding to the breakup, more interested, it seemed, in what he would do next.

When he told her, she laughed. "Tulip mania. That's what you've caught."

He winced at her reference: how, in the seventeenth century, the Dutch began investing in tulip bulbs and inflated prices to the point of madness, a single bulb costing as much as a country estate. Then it all collapsed. Worthless bulbs destroyed the economy.

"You don't have to worry about me," he told her. "I won't ruin the country. They'll hardly know I'm there."

•

He spent the afternoon trying to study flower catalogues, to immerse in the colorful pages, imagining what it would be like when he owned a garden of his own, a small plot on the broad flat landscape. Spreading open the slick paper, he leaned close to the photos, as if to inhale scents, unable to blot out the image of Tat's feet, the urgency of his impulse. He had expected an ideal cleanliness in Holland, a sense of precise control.

In the evening, after he ate, Russell watched the reflected streetlights rippling on the canal. Windows glowed in the houses around him. Tat still had her doors wide open, but her space was dark and she was nowhere in sight.

He went into his bedroom and stared at himself in the mirror on the wardrobe door, patting his face with both hands, rubbing his cheekbones and the line of his jaw. His age surprised him, the creases in his brow, the loose flesh under his chin.

The evening before his flight to Amsterdam, Russell shaved the beard he had worn half his life, black when it first grew in, almost all grey when he snipped away clumps with a small sewing scissors. Next he had lathered thickly and hacked at the stubble with abrupt razor strokes, wondering all the time why he was doing this. At the end his skin stung as if he had scraped it raw.

Now, the soreness gone, he gazed at the reflection, as if rediscovering someone he had known many years before.

•

The day was hot again, unusual weather for the city, the people in the shops told him when he bought food. Dressed in shorts and a tee shirt, embarrassed to look down at his thin, pale legs, Russell tried to blot the humidity from his face with a damp towel. He stood at an open window, wrapping the cloth around his forehead, envisioning what he could plant where the sunlight was brightest, irritated by the weeds growing between the bricks of the courtyard.

Driven to pull them out, to make everything neat, he hurried down the stairs and squatted, tearing up weeds by the fistful, alternating hands, tossing the roots against a wall. As fast as he worked, he realized the job would take days with a courtyard of that size, hundreds of bricks set into the dirt. But after an hour in the humid heat, saturated with sweat, dizzy, Russell paused to sit back, crossed his arms on his knees, and cradled his head, listening to the shrill squawking of the gulls that hovered over the canals.

Then an animal shrieked, a sound so piercing that Russell leaped up, certain the creature was in great pain. But he saw nothing until the black and white cat writhed between the bars of the fence and began licking itself, bending its head down deep between its hind legs. When Russell moved toward it, the cat darted into its apartment window.

At that moment Tat unlatched the gate and pushed her bicycle into the courtyard, the paint on its frame red and chipped like the polish on her toenails. "What happened to the cat?" he called to her.

"Cat? What cat?"

"It sounded like it was in agony." "

Oh, cats are always screaming."

"Not like that." For an instant Russell suspected that she had done something terrible to the creature, something deliberately cruel.

She gave him a thin smile. "Do you always worry so much about dumb animals?"

"Oh, I fuss over everything." Janice had accused him of that during a quarrel, standing a foot away and screaming: "What good is it? All your bother? Your washing and your weeding? It changes nothing. You're useless!"

Tat wheeled the bike closer until she stood beside him, her feet covered by canvas shoes, so white they seemed newly bought, as if she had read his thoughts. "I'm not like that at all," she said. "I let other people worry about me."

"Then you should get a cat to protect you from the rats."

"I hate cats." She said it lightly, showing her teeth. Yesterday, when he first saw her, in her panic, he had found her attractive, but now he considered her plain, with a wide face and a coarse nose.

Russell felt a warmth against his bare leg and looked down to see the black and white cat. But when he bent to pet it, it hissed, pulled back its ears, and swiped out with a paw.

"So much for your caring," Tat said. She shoved the bicycle into the rack and unlocked her door.

•

After he showered, Russell wrote cards to his children, the same photo of the canals, the same message to each—the city was wonderful, he was delighted to be here, he hoped they would visit, unable to picture any one of them sitting in this room with him. On an impulse, he uncapped his pen and scrawled Janice's address, the one that had been his for years: "Still settling in and eager to begin my horticultural studies." In the tense quiet after the divorce hearing, the lawyers still in the room, she had scorned his future: "You don't know *anything* about flowers. Whatever you touch will die." He imagined her ripping the card, the vein in her neck pulsating, her face purple.

•

An hour before twilight, when the air cooled, Russell began walking the streets of Leiden, along the Rapenburg canal to the narrow lanes around the Pieterskerk, past the town hall on Bree straat, over the bridge that crossed the Nieuwe Rijn canal to the hill of the Burcht, along Haarlemmer straat. A steady flow of cyclists streamed past him, calm, taking their time. At the outdoor cafes at the water's edge, sat students from the university, young and friendly, sharing good spirits. Alone, aware that the world was offering a very pleasant city, Russell did not know how to make himself a part of it.

As he turned toward home in the darkness along the canal behind Hoge Woerd straat, a bicycle passed him, pedaled by a man in a black turtleneck, a woman poised on the back fender, wearing a cocktail dress, high heels, and a strand of pearls. The tires were wobbling, the fenders clattering. When the wheels hit a gap in the stone, the woman let out a high-pitched squeal, as if drunk. Russell felt sure it was Tat, called her name in a greeting. As the bicycle disappeared, the woman raised her hand, but he couldn't tell whether it was a wave or a gesture for balance.

•

"What are you doing here?" Tat asked Russell the next time he saw her, stepping close behind him while he weeded the bricks, startling him with the sound of her voice. She repeated her question, louder this time, as if speaking to a deaf man.

"Tulips," he told her, explained himself briefly, unwilling to reveal too much, to have her mock him as Marci did.

"So you are a lover of beauty," she said.

"And you? Do you like flowers?"

"They die too fast. A week of blooming and then they shrivel. I prefer green vines. Thick sap."

"And where do you find them?" Russell suspected she was taunting him, making it up as she spoke.

"The Botanical Gardens. You find everything there. Flowers for you, vines for me. Something for everybody." She smiled clenched teeth. "We live in such an ideal place."

•

After breakfast he walked to the Botanical Gardens, but missed the entrance set back off Rapenburg straat, trying to read his map and blundering into dead ends. He spent ten minutes searching for a gate, annoyed at his inability to find something so simple. Once inside, he strolled the paths, gazing at trees and shrubs and plants gathered from throughout the world, thick leaves from Africa, delicate branches from Asia, studying the plaques with their Latin names, shaken by the extent of his ignorance. Here, in another country, he knew that Janice was right. Flowers had been the first excuse he could conjure to get away.

He stepped into a greenhouse, its air hung heavy with mist. The thick odor of vegetation cloyed, and he had to breathe through his mouth, almost gasping.

Someone spoke, a sharp "Nein," German, not Dutch, and he heard a sound like a slap, then a groan. When he turned a corner, back at the rear of the greenhouse, behind broad-leaved palms in massive wooden containers, he saw Tat and a man in what seemed to be an embrace, the man shorter, swollen with muscles, his arms tight around her, pushing her against a table. But her fists were clenched behind his back, her jaw locked in a grimace. The man had his mouth at her ear, whispering harsh sounds Russell could not comprehend.

"Tat," he called, about to rush beside her, to pull her free.

She shook her head furiously. "Get away! Stop following me!"

Russell hesitated, arms raised, still ready to step forward. But when the man, pale-haired and red-faced, turned to glare at him, shouting a guttural curse, he backed away and fled the greenhouse, out into the sweet smell of the garden.

•

In his apartment, through the rest of the day, he kept pacing from the sofa to the window, looking for a sign that she had returned, thinking how sparsely he was living. The apartment offered only a few shelves and a narrow wardrobe; he had to store half his clothes inside two suitcases propped against a corner. The more time he spent there, the more dislocated he felt.

He waited up half the night, eating only a slab of cheese, slicing precise cubes with a paring knife, not turning on a lamp, staring at the canal, watching the lights of the city go out one by one. Still there was no sign of her. But when he awoke in the morning, stiff and cramped, Tat sat in the courtyard, lounging on a plastic chair in pink shorts, her thick white legs stretched full length. Wide wraparound sunglasses covered half her face. Russell felt sure he would expose a bruised swelling if he reached out and lifted them.

He stood in the doorway looking over the courtyard, not sure if he should approach her, then kneeled to beckon the grey cat. It yawned, stretched, and moved slowly toward him to rub its face against his palm. Russell stroked the fur under its chin and heard purring.

"It always flees from me. Terrified." Tat crossed her legs and leaned forward as if huddling in her chair.

"That's because it knows you hate cats," he said, still kneeling, running an open hand along the length of the animal's coat.

"I'm not a friendly person."

Russell rose to approach her, and the cat drew back against a wall. "I wasn't following you yesterday."

"It doesn't matter."

"Are you all right?"

He stared down at her sunglasses and saw two elongated reflections of his face.

"I'm absolutely wonderful." She hissed the words.

"Can I do anything?"

"Why don't you spend your time enjoying the historic sights of the city? Your Pilgrims lived here before they escaped to the New World. Walk in their footsteps."

"I came to discover my future, not my past."

Tat clenched the arms of her chair. "Then watch where you look."

•

Russell should have been visiting the bulb fields, reading, interviewing experts, forcing himself to do what he came for. He had so much to learn— soils, temperatures, nutrients, drainage, species, hybrids. So much. Instead he lay awake choking back anger over Tat's rejection, telling himself he was a fool for caring. He had no rights in her life. She didn't attract him. But he found himself drawn to the window to catch sight of her, to see if her bicycle stood in its rack, if her light burned.

•

Long past midnight, as Russell watched, her door banged open, Tat and the man wedged into the tight space, both her hands pushing against his chest, as if trying to force him out, he much more powerful, digging fingers into her shoulder. She thrashed against him, her pink robe parting to expose pale flesh. Russell called out, "No!" Then the man wrapped an arm about her waist and pulled the door shut with his other hand. The slam echoed in the darkness.

Russell dressed hurriedly, his sweatshirt inside out, shoes without socks. Down in the courtyard, he leaned against her wall even though he knew the stone would deaden all sound. He heard only the soft splash of water at the edge of the canal. When he closed his hand on the doorknob, he knew he would not turn it, certain she would curse his meddling.

•

In late morning when Russell returned from the shops with food for the day, an express packet jutted from his mail slot, bold print announcing U.S. Mail. Though his heart pounded, he didn't open it until he had stored his groceries and sat on the sofa holding the envelope in his fingers, trying to imagine what could be inside.

Finally he made himself pull back the flap and slid out a smaller envelope, this one embossed with Janice's name. He read her letter, confused by many words that seemed just ink smears. Usually he could decipher her writing, but this seemed to have been dashed in distress, her hand shaking.

Finally, he understood. Marci's husband had abandoned her for someone else, another woman from the office. Devastated, their daughter had quit her job and come home to Janice, back to the room of her childhood, unable to sleep, weeping in the darkness.

Russell's first reaction was to think that, at least, he hadn't left for love or sex, or whatever it was that made people desperate for each other. That was the last thing he wanted now. He knew he should call but couldn't, unwilling to hear their voices, fearful one of them, ex-wife or daughter, would insist that he fly home. What good could he do either of them? He would enter a room, embrace his daughter and speak clichés—that her despair was only temporary, that she soon would be happy again. Then he saw himself standing in silence, Marci still miserable, Janice glowering from across the room. He tried to write a reply, tearing each attempt, frustrated at the foolishness of his words. Finally, he jotted a note, asking Janice to tell Marci he loved her, struck by the realization that loving a child didn't mean you could fix her life.

At the post office, clutching the letter at the mail slot, he considered telling Tat—the only person he knew in this city—of his daughter's plight, then imagined her scornful response, her insistence that nothing about him mattered to her. If she laughed, he would hit her. The sensation of the blow tingled in his hand.

•

When he returned from mailing, unsure what else he should have said, Russell heard Tat's swearing, harsh words in a strange language. He looked out to see her swerving her bicycle over the courtyard, chasing both cats, the animals scurrying away from her and then stopping just beyond her wheels as if taunting. Her shouts became fiercer, her pedaling more frantic, until she was spinning in circles and kicking out each time she neared one of the animals. She dropped the bicycle, clanging metal, and chased them on foot, knocking over the plastic chairs, trying to pry bricks from the dirt. When both cats hopped back inside their window, she sat in the middle of the courtyard and shouted furiously.

"Leave those cats alone!" he cried. She called something back, sounds he knew were a curse. He rushed out his door, unable to control his anger, but by the time he got down the stairs, she was gone, the fence gate wide open, her back wheel flashing out of sight.

He reached down for a stone and threw it at the wall of her structure, as hard as he could, breathless, dizzy from the effort. Then it struck him: he didn't even like her.

•

After darkness when she still had not returned, Russell felt compelled to search the city, though he had no idea where to look. She could be anyplace. But he had to get away from the apartment, from the window that looked out to her door.

Outside, lights illuminated the church steeples, danced on the surface of the canals. Along Niewe Rijn workers prepared stalls for the next morning's produce market. Despite the late hour, people strolled the sidewalks beside the water, men and women with arms linked, happy voices, soft laughter. For an instant Russell shuddered with an urge to knock them over the embankment.

In a narrow lane near the Pieterskerk he sat outside a cafe and ordered a beer. At the other tables people were still eating. Beside him a young couple rocked a baby in a stroller, pink skin and fine blond hair. The child smiled up at him and Russell stared back, bewildered by its attention.

Russell heard a chair scrape on the cobblestones and turned to watch a man take a seat several tables away, moving slowly, thick-necked, muscles tensed across wide shoulders. Under the dim bulbs of the lane, his face was pale, his cropped hair looking bleached, artificial. It was Tat's man. Russell was certain of it. He closed one hand about the beer bottle, clutching the chill glass in the other.

The man was older than Russell had first thought, perhaps his age, face lined, eyes set back in shadow, his jaw sharp and narrow, too small for so many teeth. While the others around them clattered silverware, lifted glasses, engrossed in conversations, the man glared at Russell, chest heaving against the taut cloth of his turtleneck. Russell took a swig of beer, held it in his mouth, unable to swallow. The man rose abruptly, swinging an arm as if striking out. The glass fell from Russell's hand. People flinched at the sharp smashing, watching in silence at the fragments that glittered on the stones. The baby burst into tears. Russell gripped the neck of the bottle until the man turned into the darkness, then rubbed cool fingertips into his forehead.

•

On his way home the streets seemed suddenly empty. He found himself shivering though the night was warm. His steps were quick, and he hunched his shoulders, expecting a force from the darkness, a blow on the back of his head. But he wouldn't look behind, plunged forward at the edge of running, ashamed that his fear was so obvious.

Even inside his building, the door double-locked, he hesitated at the foot of the stairway, looking up at the dim glow of the ceiling fixture, wondering what lay behind the curve of the wall. When he put his foot on the first riser, he told himself he would go straight into his bedroom and refuse to know if Tat were home. But he was drawn immediately to the light of her window, the flicker of shadows, certain she was not alone.

Awake through the night, dozing only for seconds, snapping his head to fight exhaustion, splashing his eyes with tap water, Russell watched for the man to emerge. Cat shapes crossed the roofs in the moonlight, crouched and stalking, as if pursuing a prey. Tat's light did not go out, and her door never opened.

•

When the sun rose, pink bands rippling across the canal, Russell roused himself from a brief dozing to cross the courtyard to her door, hesitating before he knocked. Then he knocked again, louder, with the side of his fist. "A rat," he called. "I saw a rat go in."

After the third time he knocked, he gripped the knob and shook. To his surprise, the door swung open, and he froze in the entranceway, tensed for an attack. But nothing happened. He stepped inside to a silent room, the mattress wrenched away from the wall, smothering a thin table, a lamp knocked to the floor, its shade crushed, the bulb still burning. Tat's coat lay spread on the scatter rug, arms knotted behind the back.

"Tat!" He shouted her name, as if she could be hiding in this naked space. Outside again, Russell saw that her bicycle was gone. He thought he had seen it there last night, now wasn't sure. It could have been shadows, a shape conjured by his memory.

The two cats entered Tat's room through the open door, sniffing the floor, climbing the furniture, hunching forward and curling lips at each strange scent.

•

Russell walked the street alongside the canal, eyes scanning the ground, unsure what he would find. He didn't even know Tat's last name or where she came from or how she lived. She was as foreign in Leiden as he was, another aberration.

Several blocks away, past a bridge over the water, the sidewalk ended abruptly, the concrete slabs broken into fragments and heaped in the mud beside a construction site. The canal was undergoing renovation, the street blocked by barrels and wooden barriers fixed at the edge of the water. Large sheets of rusted metal held back the embankment.

The morning began to brighten. People stirred on the other side of the water, moving inside the windows, opening doors, pushing bicycles onto the street. Vans parked outside the shops to unload boxes. A bakery was busy with customers, the bell over its door a faint tinkle in the distance. A woman slid back the covering of her flower stall, a hundred colors suddenly brilliant in the new sun.

Russell covered his face and turned away, then saw Tat's bicycle wedged between two blank walls, both tires flat, the chipped frame bent, the chain off its sprocket. He stood frozen, with no idea where to take it, who to tell, what to say.

Russell's gaze followed the reaches of the canal, the twist of its vanishing behind a row of buildings. He made himself step into the dirt at the edge of the water. But he closed his eyes, unable to look, shuddering at what he might find. With a gasp, he forced himself to stare down and saw nothing but a brown murk. People passed, more and more, moving rapidly, eager to begin another day in the life of this city. None paid him attention, a man in the shadows, alone.

MISSING VENICE

A FEW MINUTES OUT OF PADUA, David dozed into a nightmare that they had missed Venice and, after hours of barely creeping, were suddenly hurtling toward the Adriatic. He felt himself grabbing at suitcases, struggling with the compartment door, desperate to jump from the train and pull Virginia after him, certain that if they did not escape at once, they would plummet into oblivion.

But at a metallic shriek he opened his eyes to iron pipe intestines, the thumping percussion of factories, smokestack fires that seared the darkness. The train lay at a dead stop in Mestre, stalled, as if it would never cross the last kilometers to Venice.

And it wasn't Virginia beside him despite all their months of anticipation, but Donny instead, his son, an oversized fourteen-year-old slouched on the seat, scowling at the flames in the window, kicking unlaced sneakers against a metal panel. The boy hadn't said a word the entire thirteen hours of the trip, through the excruciating pace, the endless delays. He didn't speak; he didn't read; he didn't even listen to his iPod; he just shoved hands deep into his pockets and oozed hostility.

But Maria hadn't shut up since they left the Stazione Termini in Rome. Plump and pockmarked, her shape reminded David of a miniature Donny, through she was a woman in her thirties, an absolute stranger until the middle of that day.

Heavy-lidded, David rubbed hard at his face, fighting off sleep. Maria grinned at his return to consciousness without a hitch in the story she was droning to her son, even though the boy gave no sign of paying attention, something about panic in Tangier, her passport sliding down behind her suitcase lining.

She had stumbled into the compartment, hours ago, just as the train was building momentum to leave Rome, huffing, grinning, baggage spewing from under her arms, off her shoulders.

The trip had begun extremely late, David fuming in his confusion,

Donny lagging like dead weight. They stood on a platform for hours, David peering down the empty track, pacing among the heaped suitcases trying to get someone in the crowd of shrugging Italians to explain what had happened to the 8 a.m. Venice express, while Donny muttered curses and stuffed his mouth with candy bars. At 11 a train appeared, and David scrambled aboard, dragging his baggage and his son after him, only to sit for another hour until the creaking start and Maria's breathless arrival.

She was the one to tell them about the one-day railway workers' strike. "We're all victims of a slowdown": the first words out of her mouth, then a non-stop rush, all the time the train inched over countryside, in and out of cities, across a barren brown landscape. Despite her chatter, David sensed that she was as miserable as the boy, her animation a desperate thrashing against a flood of gloom. All day he had felt the compartment sinking, as if the two of them were pulling him under.

To save himself, he gripped the armrest, imagined he was holding Virginia's hand, stroking the soft flesh, blood surging at her warmth. His fantasy of their being alone in a compartment, reaching over to draw a darkening shade and touching his lips to a smooth tanned shoulder. His wife at last, his new life finally begun. For months they had dreamed of being dazzled by the sunset on the Grand Canal, never considering that they could be an ocean apart, her tickets transferred to a son he barely knew.

"We're in Mestre," Maria said as David blinked his way back to comprehension. "It has a population of 75,000 and manufactures chemicals and heavy metals." Her head was a guidebook. "Pollution from Mestre is a serious problem for Venice. It's in the air, eating into the stucco."

David sighed, long and deep, almost a groan. The last thing he needed on this train was a pathetic lab technician from Santiago compelled to render every detail of every place she had visited during a two-month round-the-world once-in-a-lifetime holiday: the goiter of the woman who rented rooms in Macao, the cockroach found in a cafeteria meal on the Boul' Mich'. Short, squat, fat-faced. He couldn't imagine any man fantasizing about her in a locked compartment.

While David watched his son's eyelids droop and his head slump against the seatback, Maria renewed her outrage about the price of single rooms. "Some hotels charge me for a double even though I only use one bed. Can you believe that?" Her English jarred, with long vowels and trilled r's.

"It must be a problem travelling alone." David swallowed a yawn.

"I live alone. I'm alone most of the time."

The train stirred with a vibration that sent a tremor through the compartment. In his chest David felt the engine strain to break the inertia. He grunted as they lurched forward. Donny turned his face into the cushion and smacked a fist against the metal wall.

"Your son is exhausted," Maria said, then asked, "Do you have other children?" one of the rare moments she did not talk about herself.

David shook his head.

"Will his mother be waiting for you in Venice?"

"His mother is having a baby."

Her mouth dropped.

"His mother is not my wife. Not now. Not for years." David glanced at Donny to see if he was listening, but the boy had an arm around his head, fingers twisted in the hacked ends of a haircut he had given himself.

"I'm married to someone else now." David summoned up a picture of Virginia, soft and slim, lovely in summer dresses. It gave him great pleasure just to watch her move. But he couldn't shut out the memory of the anger that twisted her face: "The reservations are paid for. Nonrefundable. He's your son. Just take him and go."

"And she's in Venice," Maria said, half statement, half question.

"She's back home too."

Maria knotted her brow.

"Look," he said, exasperated. "It's not a big deal. His mother asked me to watch after him for while. She's going to have to adjust to a baby. It's a tough time for everybody."

It had been hell, a night of phones ringing long past midnight, Lucy ranting long distance, Virginia weeping bitterly in the living room, irate women in both his ears. "You bailed out ten years ago," Lucy kept screaming. "Now you see him once a year and stuff him with ice cream. He's infantile. He destroys things. He wants to ruin my marriage. My life! He says he hates my baby! I want him out of here!"

All this three days before their flight, Virginia's suitcase spread open in the guest room, half packed with new clothes, guidebooks and brochures scattered across the carpet. And now beside him a son from half a continent away materialized at an airport gate, off one plane and hauled onto another, a sloppy kid with a smeared chin in a filthy outgrown sweatsuit.

Instead of a greeting, he had glared at David and said, "The bitch can shove that baby back where it came from."

"It's nice that you're such a good father," Maria said, and the train lurched.

Finally, at 1:17 a.m. on the station clock, they arrived in Venice. David stirred himself to unfold two chrome luggage carts and strap down suitcases. Maria collected an assortment of canvas bags. Every time she grabbed one, she seemed to drop another. When David offered help, she grinned thanks and let him pick up after her.

For weeks he had anticipated sharing Virginia's awed reaction to discovering Venice. He deliberately had planned their schedule to arrive in early evening in time to change, stroll to an outdoor meal in the Piazza San Marco, and await the sunset. Now it was the middle of the night, Maria squealing at Donny to catch her umbrella.

They emerged from the station into a grey night under a cloud-covered quarter moon. The area was dingy, a row of tiny hotels with faint signs and loiterers slouching in the shadows. They had to wait for a vaporetto in a white shed bobbing at the water's edge. David rolled the two suitcases down a wooden walkway, Maria's heaviest duffle bag over his shoulder. Donny sank onto one of the slat benches, eyes puffed with fatigue.

Whichever direction David looked, up or down the canal, the view was drab, except for the small gold-domed church directly across a slice of water. Maria, seated beside him on the bench, already had her green Michelin guide open. "Fondamente Saint Simeon Piccolo," she said. "There are 190 churches in Venice, nearly all interesting. But I can't find any details about this one." Under a weak bulb she squinted at the page with disappointment.

Aside from two grizzle-faced vaporetto employees smoking cigarettes down to their fingertips, the only others in the waiting shed were three young people, a muscular male in a black turtleneck and faded overalls and two women, one curly headed and round, the other tall and dark, with pitch black hair, drawn cheeks, and stark facial bones. She wore a tank top, long dark legs emerging from cutoff shorts. The night was chilly enough for David to button his sweater. But she did not shiver once.

All three were either drunk or stoned, with arms wrapped around each other, breaking out into snatches of songs, their speech chanted in a language he had trouble placing. It might have been Italian, but with harsh Germanic intonations. The dark woman's loud hoarse voice dominated, as she orchestrated each sound with an angular hand gesture. Every minute or so, at her lead, the three wailed, "Oh, mama!"

Maria grinned at their antics, nudged Donny to make him look, as if the three were putting on a show just for them. But he turned away and spit at the water. David imagined the male suddenly stomping across the planks and knocking Donny into the canal, the boy flailing in a ridiculous splash, then sinking like a stone. A shadow fell across the man's face like a scar, and David swallowed.

When the plump woman gave her the edge of a smile, Maria took that as an excuse to approach and admire the jagged bronze pendant the dark woman wore against her breastbone. The three stared blankly at her English. She tried again in Spanish. After a silence, when the smoking workers halted their conversation to stare, the dark woman glared and did a jerky, arm-flapping dance step that forced Maria backwards. She slunk to the bench and looked to David for solace. But he pretended he had not seen a thing. He caught Donny glancing at him, face screwed in a smirk.

It was another ten minutes before the vaporetto came. By then Maria had located the stop for David's hotel, Campo Santa Maria del Giglio, in her guidebook. His travel agent had made reservations at what she called "a congenial but inexpensive little place" called the Villa Giorgione. He and Virginia had saved for a year; then Lucy's lawyer sent the bill for Donny's therapy, and Virginia had urged him to cancel. But David had insisted that they owed this trip to themselves; he wasn't going to let the son of a failed marriage ruin their future. And now on a chill night at the fringe of Venice he could taste the folly of his decision.

David loaded Maria's suitcases on board and gave her his hand as she stepped down onto the deck. Donny waved off his help. The three young people, without luggage, waited until the boat started to pull away and jumped on with screaming leaps. Maria shrank against David each time a pair of feet pounded the deck.

When the boat began to move, churning out a white wake on the empty canal, she was smiling again, guessing the names of the palaces on the water's edge as if she had memorized the map. Palazzo Grimani, Palazzo Rezzonio, Palazzo Pesaro.

David saw only facades and doorways, silhouettes of roofs and domes, low grey shapes of moored motor launches. He turned and realized that Donny had slipped inside the cabin and collapsed onto a bench, eyes closed, mouth open, chin bouncing against his chest with the vibrations of the boat.

Maria startled him with a nudge and a question. "What is your boy's mother's name?"

"Lucy." It felt odd to be speaking that name here, on a canal in Venice.

"Why did you leave her?"

"I didn't love her."

Her face took on its blank expression. "Is love so important?"

David squeezed his hands around the chill railing. "You wouldn't understand."

"And the boy?"

"He was a baby then."

"What is he now?"

"Listen! I didn't make him this way. He lives with his mother."

Maria looked toward the cabin and gasped. The three young people were hovering over Donny, rising on tiptoes, wriggling fingers. David couldn't hear over the engine noise, but he thought they were chanting.

When he rushed inside, they sprawled across the bench on the other side, arms folded and glaring. He shook Donny; the boy wouldn't open his eyes. "You okay?" David said. "They're assholes," Donny muttered. David grasped his shoulders to make him move outside, away from them.

He heard Maria cry, "We're here!"

The vaporetto eased toward a pier marked with the name of their stop. David hoisted Donny and hurried to gather their suitcases, leaving Maria to fend for herself. The three young people shook open hands at them and called, "Oh, mama!"

On the pier, luggage at her feet, Maria gazed helplessly and wondered if she could find a room at David's hotel. He shrugged and told her to try.

They moved through a narrow pathway between building fronts and found themselves on a cobblestone street. Maria consulted her map and pointed ahead. In a minute they moved through an open square deserted of people, the wheels of their luggage rattling over the stones.

The Hotel Giorgione was small and neat. Maria peered inside and said its lobby seemed very nice. When David pulled at the door, it was locked. His watch read past two a.m. He rapped on the glass until a clerk appeared, a bald man with a cardigan sweater under his suit jacket. He unlocked and held the door open a crack. David identified himself, and the clerk shrugged. "We have no rooms, signore."

"I made a reservation. I sent a deposit."

"I remember your name, signore. But your deposit never arrived. We could not hold the room without it."

David wanted to hit the man, slap his thick brown glasses across the lobby.

"Listen! It's the middle of the night. We're exhausted. I gave my travel agent a check six goddamn weeks ago!" Donny sat on the cobblestone and sprawled back against a suitcase. Maria just listened, as if storing away another anecdote.

"I can do nothing, signore." The clerk withdrew and quickly bolted the door, leaving them outside.

David had an urge to stand in the middle of the campo and roar frustration, bellow until he woke up every sleeping soul in Venice.

"I wonder what we'll do," Maria said, looking up at him with her thick face as if the three of them were a unit.

He tried to speak calmly. "Let's just find San Marco. There's got to be something there."

David made Donny drag one suitcase, Maria the other. He lugged her collection of bags, straps over both shoulders, handles in the crooks of his arms, up and down the steps of bridges that seemed to cross and re-cross the same winding canal. With no streetlights, with the moon buried in cloud, the darkness swallowed them. He knew they were lost, wandering randomly in a city of strangers.

They finally saw other people, a couple, two young lovers hand in hand, sitting on church steps. In broken English, on a pocket map under a penlight, the couple traced a route back the way they had come, but when they moved away David couldn't remember any of it.

He decided to follow a single street wherever it led. In front of a small hotel with a polished wooden door a group of drunken men stopped their singing to swarm about Maria, crooning Italian endearments. One dropped to his knees and seized her hand, smacked a kiss on her knuckles. Another stroked her hair. She just stood in the middle of them grinning foolishly. Although his instinct was to abandon her, David pushed through, seized her arm, and pulled her away.

"Arrivederci," the men chanted after them, "Arrivederci," and dissolved into laughter. Donny started laughing too, just as loudly, the first amusement he had shown since David found him staring at a wall in the airport.

Maria dropped the suitcase and ran off, shoes pounding at the stones with heavy steps. At the first side street, no more than an alley, she swerved and disappeared.

Still burdened with her baggage, David seized Donny's shoulders and shook, suddenly furious. "You humiliated her."

"What about those guys?"

"All day she tried to be nice to you."

"She's an ugly pig."

David slapped him, felt the sting radiate up through his arm. The boy stared back, refusing to admit pain. Then David calmed. "You take both carts and follow me."

With Maria's bags bulging at his side, David could barely fit into the alley. He considered dropping them, then wondered if he'd been able to find his way back, if they would still be there.

It was a long passageway, windowless outer walls looming on both sides, warehouses perhaps or factories, built by people who didn't care about light. He turned back to made sure Donny was trudging behind with the carts. Their rumbling seemed muffled now.

He saw a sliver ahead, not really a light, just a shaft of grey glow less dense than the darkness. This is ugly, he kept thinking, bleak and ugly. On an ugly street on an ugly night seeking a ugly women followed by his ugly son.

And now he understood why he had made this trip—to take Donny far from Virginia, fleeing from fear that knowing his son would make her realize she would never find the life she had hoped for in him.

Then he stumbled over something soft, and the heft of the baggage toppled him forward until he sprawled across a tiny square at the end of the alley, a place barely wider than the length of his body. When he pulled himself up, he saw Maria huddled against a brick wall, her arms wrapped around her ankles, her face pressed deep between her knees. He had tripped over her.

In a few seconds he realized the strange yowling noise was her sobbing, a crying unlike any he had ever heard before, a terrible animal misery.

"What's wrong?" he asked, though he was too exhausted to care.

"It's so awful."

"What?"

"Everything." And she fell into an even louder wailing.

David began to reach out, as if there were no choice but to comfort her. But something stepped on his hand. He yelled and looked up at the thin bare leg of the woman from the vaporetto. She was wearing spiked heels. When he tried to pull his hand free, she shifted her weight and the jagged pendant dangled over him.

"Hey? What're you doing?"

She gestured back toward the darkness with her chin, and the others appeared, the round woman, the man in the turtleneck. Something glinted in his hand.

The round woman seized Maria's hair and pulled her head back, arching her neck, shouting something, a single harsh word over and over again. David expected the man to swipe out and slash across her throat, blood to suddenly spurt over them all.

"Do you want money?" he made himself plead. "Credit cards?"

The man reached down and seized David by the back of the head and yanked him upward until they were face to face, grinding his nose into David's cheek. He reeked of a sweet aftershave like an ointment on his skin.

This is death, David thought, and the sensation of an absolute emptiness shuddered through him.

"Bastards! Goddamn fucking bastards!" Donny lunged toward them swinging a suitcase in a wide circle, thumping the man behind the knees, knocking his legs out from under him. The man tumbled atop David, then scrambled off into the alley. The two women backed against a wall, kicking and pointing at Donny, twisting their hands into some obscene gesture.

When the boy stood panting in the square, they screamed convulsively, the man too, next to them now, the three of them shaking their arms in the identical gesture. Then the tall woman did her jerky dance and spit at Maria. The three spun and ran into the darkness, roaring "Oh, mama!" again and again.

Donny tried to hurl the luggage after them. It crashed on the cobblestones, splitting open and spewing clothing. David stared, trying to recognize each item, which of the twisted garments was his and which was his son's. When he turned, Donny was beside Maria, the two of them clasping each other, sobbing and clinging, as if their grief was endless.

Through the space between two buildings, past the tiled roofs, David could make out a narrow view, the glittering edge of a golden dome, a slice of distant sea. And he knew that whatever happened next, he was seeing as much of Venice as would ever matter to him. For months, Virginia had memorized a city from picture books—churches, squares, and palaces. But he had found another Venice, nothing like the one she had dreamed. He felt so sad for her that he wanted to weep.

Then he sensed the swelling of his hand. Something is broken, he thought. David touched the purple flesh with a fingertip and suddenly reeled. He cried out, blinded by the intensity of his pain. Through the tear blur he saw his son reaching up to him as if they were bound by a single hurt.

POACHING

WHEN HE SAW VALERIE'S CAR PARKED BEHIND THE INN, Dennis felt a great relief. Despite her promises over the phone, he hadn't really believed she would show up. It was only four but already dark on this January afternoon. As he pulled into a space three down from her car, he realized she was still sitting in the driver's seat. He rushed over and pulled open her door, eager to embrace her. She did not get out, pointing past him.

"I'm late," he apologized. "I even left work earlier than I said I would, but the traffic in the city was awful." He wouldn't ask when she left, not wanting to remind her what she had done, assuming she had begun her drive minutes after James and the boys set off on their fishing trip.

"Look," she said, still pointing. Dennis followed her fingertips, tilting his head to gaze upward.

"Have you ever seen stars like that?"

Thousands glittered in a clear sky, shapes of constellations whose names he had forgotten, stars in every direction, arcing past the tall trees at the edge of the village. For an instant they made him uneasy, so many, overwhelming. Then he thought to say, "It's being out in the country. Beautiful. We made a brilliant choice." They had chosen the inn from a guide, in a place where they knew no one, where no one would know them.

Dennis offered a hand, tentative, like a test, half expecting her to shake her head, pull the door shut, and drive off. He held his breath until she let him guide her out onto the gravel drive. He wrapped arms around her, and she fell into his embrace with a sob. He looked at her face, the glint of her blue eyes, first thinking they reflected the stars, then realizing it was the light over the inn's sign. She kissed him, long and deep, his hand in her hair, her fingertips touching his face. Finally, Valerie whispered. "It's chilly. Why don't we go inside?"

He breathed the scent of a fireplace, saw chimney smoke wafting over the thatched roof. "It looks cozy."

They had only overnight bags, and Dennis carried both. At the desk he signed his name and address on the registration card, listing only his car make and license plate number. A very young clerk, the owner's teenage daughter Dennis assumed, welcomed them with a smile and handed him a key linked to a wooden block engraved with the room number.

Up a flight of stairs, back along a dim corridor, he led the way to the room. Hands trembling, he unlocked the door and flipped the light switch. All the furnishings looked antique, the wooden chest, the four-poster bed with a quilted spread, the tin lamp in the beamed ceiling. Windowpanes reflected their presence, and Valerie hurried to close the blinds.

Within seconds they were in each other's arms, pulling at their clothing, quickly naked, making love, the room alive with his moans, her gasps, the bed boards creaking. When they finally lay in a still embrace, she said, her mouth close to his ear, "They all must have heard us."

"Who's they?"

"Everyone in this inn. That girl."

"Then they're sick with envy."

Valerie took his wrist to look at his watch. It was past seven. "I can't eat here. People looking at us."

He would have liked that, others thinking they were a couple, husband and wife. But he nodded. "All right. We'll see what else is in the village."

They showered, dressed, and went down to the lobby, Valerie already out the door when he handed the room key to the girl. Dennis waited for a Secret signal, a sly smile, but the girl just nodded.

When he saw Valerie standing on the side of the road, he wrapped an arm around her and said, "Which way?"

She pointed ahead toward a cluster of cottages down a slight incline, lights glowing in their windows. Behind them, he made out the silhouettes of sheep on a hillside, unmoving in the moonlight. The air felt pure and fresh.

"Would you like to live in a place like this?" he asked, careful not to imply us, though that was his wish, the two of them away from their old lives.

"It's very pretty," she said, "but I'd feel so isolated. And it would end up boring for the children. "

Dennis didn't comment, regretting having brought up the subject, telling himself he should concentrate on this weekend and pretend that Monday would never come. He took her hand, relieved when she squeezed his fingers.

The village had no sidewalks, just a cobblestone strip at the edge of the pavement. The stone cottages were old, the roofs thatched, lace curtains in the windows, pewter and crockery arranged on the sills. Every now and then he saw the glow of a television screen and wondered how people spent their lives here, if coziness were the answer.

Valerie stopped to look up at the stars. "I can't believe how magnificent the sky is."

He leaned forward to give her a quick kiss of affection.

He noticed an outdoor lamp at the end of a narrow path to their left. "That might be something." As they approached, a brighter light flicked on, shining down on them, set off by an electric eye. They found themselves on the main road, a marker pointing toward the larger towns in both directions. But the traffic was light at this hour, occasional headlights appearing from around a bend, the vehicle rushing past and disappearing around another curve. Dennis thought they were all going too fast, in a hurry to be someplace else.

"Look," Valerie said, pointing at a signboard propped on the pavement outside an entrance alcove. "A menu. We found the village pub."

"On our own. What a team."

He pushed open the door to the alcove and then a second to the interior. They paused in the doorway to get their bearings. A man and a teen-aged boy, clearly father and son, stood behind the handles at the bar, both in jeans and blue sweatshirts. The few people seated at the tables by the fireplace turned to see who had entered. In the back, a young couple, both overweight, threw darts at the board on a wall, the man leaning against the woman, arms over her shoulders, guiding her throws. The room was thick with cigarette smoke. Valerie made a face and glanced back toward the entrance.

"We've got a no smoking room," the father said, stubbing his own cigarette in an ashtray and indicating a door to his right.

Dennis and Valerie found themselves alone among the small round tables. The father moved to an end of the bar, lifting a flap and approaching them with two cardboard menus. "Anywhere you like."

When Dennis picked a table against the back wall, the man handed them the menus and asked what they were drinking. Valerie said red wine and Dennis, after a hesitation, a pint of best bitter. The father called their orders to his son and retrieved the glasses from the bar.

To Dennis' surprise, the man pulled back a chair and sat with them. Dennis felt a jolt, invaded, violated. He tried to meet Valerie's eye, hoping for a signal to ask the man to leave; but she smiled, amused.

The father was a thin man, a wave of dark hair falling over his forehead, the sweatshirt sleeves pushed up above his elbows, a tattoo on one forearm. He touched a finger to Valerie's menu. "I'd recommend the plaice and chips. We're inland, I know, but a fresh catch was delivered this morning."

When Valerie nodded, Dennis nodded too. The father signaled his son. "Call me Will," the man said. "And the boy there is called Willie. People say he was cloned."

Valerie threw back her head. "You do look alike."

"The wife is a fair woman, and so is my daughter. Though you'd hardly know they were related. They're in the kitchen frying up your fish. We're together all the time. Work down here, sleep up there." He pointed to the ceiling.

"It must be nice to have your family around you," Valerie said.

Will grinned at her. "I call myself a lucky man." He looked at Dennis and back at her. "You two must be staying at the inn."

"How could you tell?" Valerie seemed to be enjoying the man, the country lilt to his voice, and Dennis swallowed his annoyance at sharing her attention. Even though he knew it was foolish, he tensed, as if he and Will were at the verge of a struggle, hands around each other's throats.

Will leaned forward. "I know everybody in the village. Besides, you look like city people."

"Right again," Valerie told him.

"What about your family?" Will asked. "Your children?"

Dennis almost said none, that he was a bachelor. Valerie spoke quickly, "Two. Two boys. Eight and ten." Dennis feared she would add that they were off fishing with their father, but she stopped.

"With their granny while mom and dad have a holiday." Will's words were more of a statement than a question.

"Absolutely," Dennis said, too loud he feared, not sure how Valerie would have reacted, relieved when she added, "Everyone needs a holiday."

"So you'll be here tomorrow. Saturday."

"We expect to be," Valerie told him.

"Then you're in for a treat if you want to come back."

"What's that?" Valerie asked.

"Venison." Will spoke the word proudly as if naming a treasure. "We'll have venison steak and venison stew."

"Another fresh delivery?" Dennis said.

"I suppose you could say that. Courtesy of Malcolm provisions." Will laughed out loud.

"What's that?" Valerie asked.

Will leaned forward and whispered. "Can you keep a secret?" Before they could respond, he went on. "Course, if you can't, I'll deny it and I'll be the one they believe."

"Of course, they would. We're absolute strangers. They don't know anything about us. Who we really are." Valerie signaled Dennis with the blink of an eye.

Will glanced behind him, though they were the only ones in the room. "Malcolm is the local poacher. Malcolm and his dogs. They help thin out the deer population."

"What about the police?" Valerie said.

Will laughed again. "Malcolm doesn't worry about the likes of them. Once you see the man, you'll understand why the police keep their distance." He glanced at his watch. "In fact, you may be in luck. He and Sylvie are due in tonight. I'll introduce you."

Willie brought the plates, heaps of chips spilling over large plaice fillets. Will stood up. "I'll let you enjoy your dinners. Another drink?"

Valerie handed him her wine glass, but Dennis indicated that he was fine.

"Do you really want to meet Malcolm?" he said when they were alone.

"Of course. I've never met a poacher before. In fact, I thought they only existed in Victorian novels."

"Have you ever eaten venison?"

"Not until tomorrow."

Her answer surprised him; he expected her sympathy for the deer, creatures he always considered delicate and beautiful. As if reading his thoughts, she added, "We're having an adventure."

He reached across the table and took her hand. "Of course we are."

She lifted her fork with the other and chewed. "This fish is quite good.

"Mrs. Will certainly knows how to cook."

Dennis nodded, sensing that Valerie was trying too hard, that her amusement at being here was an act, not for him, but for herself, an attempt to force images of her husband and sons into a dark corner of her consciousness. Forget them, he wished he could tell her. Just for these few days. Think only of me.

He picked at the edge of the fish, stabbed a chip, with no appetite, while she ate with real pleasure, little left on her plate. He noticed that her glass was almost empty.

"Would you like to walk about the village and head back to the inn?" he asked.

"I'd like another wine." She covered his hand with hers, lightly, what he took to be a gesture of affection, nothing like the clutch of desire when they embraced in the parking lot. She had calmed her passion, but for him the months since their last time together had created a store of desire he felt could never be satisfied. He wanted her to be just as desperate. Yet he put his other hand atop hers and nodded. "Of course. Let's take our time."

At the sound of Will's voice, they both looked up. "Look who's here." First, a woman followed him through the door to the no smoking room, pleasant looking, about Valerie's age, but not as well kept, Dennis thought, a bit plump, her hair tangled from the breeze. Then the man followed, so large he had to stoop to get through the entranceway, his shoulders almost the width of the space. Will barely came up to his chest, as he patted the man's back and wrapped an arm about the woman's waist. "Meet Malcolm and Sylvie."

Sylvie smiled, and Dennis saw she was missing a tooth. Malcolm nodded, his eyes penetrating, as if he were taking the measure of the two strangers. Sylvie wore a thick quilted jacket, Malcolm just a flannel shirt. Mud-crusted green rubber boots covered his calves. His steps had left a trail of brown clumps.

"You know, I never thought to ask your names." Will looked to Valerie and Dennis. She was the one who gave them, just the first. They all shook hands, Dennis struck by how small Valerie's was in Malcolm's palm, expecting his to be crushed, surprised that the huge man's clasp was so loose.

Will slid chairs over from another table, gestured Malcolm and Sylvie to sit, joining them with a backwards straddle. "I've been telling our new friends about the venison tomorrow night." Malcolm nodded.

"Are you so sure you'll get something?" Valerie asked him.

Malcolm cleared his throat. "Dead certain."

Will grinned. "Malcolm never fails. Isn't that right, Sylvie?

"Not since I've known him," she said. "And that's been fifteen years."

Willie appeared at the curve of the bar, calling his father. Will stood reluctantly. "The boy needs his dad. You people get to know another."

Admiring Valerie's earrings, Sylvie reached out to touch a dangling hoop with her fingertip. From the animation of their faces, Dennis could tell that the women liked each other, jealous because Valerie was paying attention to a stranger, uneasy because he didn't know what to say to Malcolm.

"So, you're staying at the inn," Malcolm said.

Dennis sensed the man was just as uncomfortable having to make small talk.

"I found it in a guidebook and liked the picture. And the history. They said the original section was built in the seventeenth century."

"I wouldn't know anything about that. Everything's old around here."

"Have you lived in the village all your life?"

"No place else. I can count the days I've been away on the fingers of this hand." Malcolm held it up in front of them, Dennis again amazed at the size of it, deep abrasions along the backs of his fingers.

"No desire to explore?" he said.

"There's plenty to explore in walking distance. If you know how to look, you'll find something new every day."

"You must be a very satisfied man."

"And I've got Sylvie and the kids."

Dennis expected Malcolm to smile or at least take on an expression of contentment, but his face was fixed, the muscles of his unshaven cheeks taut. Now Valerie and Sylvie were comparing wedding rings, to his surprise Sylvie's more ornate, with a cluster of small diamonds. She explained that Malcolm helped her choose it, the two of them spending an afternoon in the jewelry stores of a nearby town. The day must have been one of Malcolm's five fingers, he thought. He worried that Sylvie would ask Valerie if he had done the same, but Valerie changed the subject, asking Sylvie about her children.

"I'm the opposite of you," Dennis said to Malcolm. "Never lived anywhere but the city."

"That would drive me crazy."

"You've never visited? On one of your days?"

"Never." Malcolm shook his head. "But I've seen it on the telly. It's not for me. Sidewalks hurt my feet."

Dennis held back his smile, not sure how the man would take it. "People are different," he said, annoyed at himself for the cliché.

Malcolm placed his hand on Sylvie's shoulders. "I'd better check on the dogs." In seconds he was gone, boots squeaking on the wooden floor.

"Where are they?" Valerie asked Sylvie.

"Tied up outside. The pair of them. He won't go anywhere without them. They're good animals."

"Aren't you worried that someone might try to steal them?" Dennis said.

Sylvie laughed, genuinely amused. "If somebody tried to touch them, they'd go for his throat. People around here know better than to mess with Malcolm's dogs."

Malcolm and Will returned to the room at the same time, Malcolm through the door, Will from the bar.

"They want to hunt," Malcolm said. "It's getting to be that time."

Will's eyes brightened. "Say, I've got a great idea. Dennis, you can go out with Malcolm tonight. It'll be an unforgettable experience. Like nothing you'd ever do in the city. And Valerie, you can go with Sylvie to see a real village cottage. Theirs is one of the oldest for miles, and Sylvie keeps it authentic."

Dennis tried to catch Valerie's eye, make a gesture of no with a twist of his brow. But before he could, she mouthed "adventure" and said it was a wonderful plan, if Sylvie didn't mind.

"Brilliant." Sylvie smiled. "I can make a cup of tea and you can meet the children."

"I'd just get in Malcolm's way," Dennis said, willing to make a quick visit to the cottage and then get Valerie back to the inn.

"It'll be all right," Malcolm said.

"As long as you do exactly what Malcolm tells you the second he tells you," Will added, than forced a laugh as if he'd been joking. "And don't pet the dogs now, Dennis."

Dennis reached under the table to touch Valerie's knee, hoping she would take it as a signal to rescue him. Instead she got up and told him, "I want to hear all about it. Every detail."

Outside the pub, the two dogs wagged tails and whined happily at the sight of Malcolm even though he had only been gone for minutes. They were tan, muscular creatures, about a hundred pounds each, Dennis estimated, stiff ridges of fur rising the lengths of their backbones. Their heads were huge, long tongues flopping over sharp teeth. He imagined a steel trap clamped onto his wrist. But now they jumped at Malcolm, paws on his chest, while he pounded them with a playful forearm. For the first time, the man was smiling.

Sylvie reached into her purse for a small light with a wide beam. She pointed it at the pathway back to the cottages. "I'll have the kettle on." She and Valerie walked off side by side, Valerie calling back "Bye," clearly enjoying herself.

"This way," Malcolm told Dennis when they were gone. He waited for two cars to pass and crossed the road. Although the dogs wore chain leashes attached to choke collars, he let them loose, yet they stayed just inches from his boots. Dennis kept a few yards behind, walking in Malcolm's footsteps through the flattened weeds.

They came to a T-junction with a narrow single-track lane marked by a stone milepost with carved hands, one pointing in the direction of the closest town, the other toward the city a hundred miles away. Malcolm turned left, saying nothing. Dennis expected that the man could have taken this route blindfolded.

They made their way by moonlight. Dennis was surprised by how well he could see at this hour, trying to recall the last time he had walked in such an empty countryside. Years, it must have been, though he couldn't remember when or where.

James thrived in the outdoors, Valerie had told him once, though she never went with him. That wasn't her idea of pleasure. Dennis assumed James and their sons were already nestled in a tent pitched on the bank of a stream, eager to be up at dawn to fish for trout. What if that stream lay up ahead and Malcolm were taking him there? He pictured Malcolm pulling back a tent flap and announcing, This man is trying to steal your wife.

An angry screeching made him stop dead in his tracks. He turned toward the sound and saw two white geese behind a wire fence, feathers quivering, furious at the intrusion. He expected the dogs to go for them, Malcolm to shout, but both man and dogs paid no intention.

"Here," Malcolm said a few yards ahead, pushing his way through a thick hedge off the lane onto a soft footpath. Dennis could feel his shoes sinking into mud, the only pair he had brought, expecting to spend the whole weekend in a room with Valerie, hours and hours of lovemaking. Now he'd be leaning over the toilet, scraping off mud.

They must have walked for fifteen minutes, Dennis hurrying to keep pace with Malcolm's long strides, the dogs with their noses to the dirt, eager for the right scent. When Dennis looked behind, he could see the shape of the church steeple pointing up at the stars and made out the faint glow of lights from the cottages. He wondered if Valerie was in one of them, sitting in a chair by the fire, a teacup in her hand, Sylvie and Malcolm's children stretched out on a rug beside them, perhaps one on Sylvie's lap, the women at peace in each other's company, Valerie telling about her own sons, how much she loved them, so deep into her visit that she had forgotten all about him.

Malcolm stopped him short with a hand in his chest and a signal to be quiet, to stay still. They had come to the edge of a tangled grove of trees, trunks tumbled and uprooted, jagged branches dangling loose and splayed across the dirt, the air thick with the scent of rotting vegetation, everything ghostly pale in the moonlight. He realized how chill the night had become, how cold he was. I'm lost, he thought. I've lost.

The dogs crouched, their haunches quivering. Malcolm breathed deep and fast. Dennis saw the shape of an animal in the midst of the trees. He felt an urge to shout, Run, Get away, but held himself as silent as Malcolm and the dogs. Then Malcolm made a sound like a growl, and the dogs bolted with loud yips. Dennis wouldn't look, couldn't, but he sensed Malcolm's excitement pulsating in the air about them. He heard the dogs' paws crushing leaves and twigs, the roars of their barking.

When a scream of terror ripped through the night, he felt as if he were being split apart and something torn from the heart of him.

FREEDOM

DROGIC RECOILED AT THE SOUNDS OF SHOTS fired into the sky from across the square, blinked at the brilliant flares of gunpowder. The city swarmed with celebration as the taxi drove him from his office to the airport, people surging over the streets in a din of voices, some wrapping arms around each other's waists as they chanted patriotic songs. The taxi could barely creep across the cobblestone square, but the driver beat a rhythm on his horn and grinned at the cheers, gripping the hands thrust through the open window.

The young were exuberant, rocking against the vehicle as if to lift it from the road. They climbed atop trams and statues, bare-chested young men waving huge flags of the republic, the women clinging to them, toasting the evening sky with bottles of wine. The elderly stood in silent weeping, some with eyes lowered in prayer.

Drogic searched the thousands of faces for his sons, boys of fourteen and fifteen who were sure to be in the midst of the crowd. He hadn't seen them in several weeks. His work kept him very busy, often traveling for days at a time, and their mother did not encourage visits. When they were with him, all his sons talked was a night such as this, craving freedom like a religion. They had shown him their weapons, rifles with chipped stocks several wars old, hidden under a roll of blankets in a shed. "What will you do with them?" he had asked. "Shoot whoever we have to," they had said, one speaking the words, the other nodding solemnly, thin boys, barely shaving, undersized for their ages.

"A great night," the driver said.

Drogic nodded. "Yes."

"How can you bring yourself to leave at a time like this?"

"Someone has to do business no matter how the times are."

"Better you than me, friend. Once I get you to the airport, I'm going to celebrate for a week."

People slapped the taxi windows, waving at Drogic, saluting him as if

he had done something heroic. He peered back into the throng, seeking
his sons.

●

By the time Drogic landed in a northern country, retrieved luggage, and
stepped out into the immaculate terminal, newspaper headlines screamed
that his city had been invaded. He snatched up copies in German, French,
English, but they all gave the same meager information: tanks had crossed
the border to fill the central square. People were in hiding. Drogic tried to
imagine the scene—panicked flight, smashed glass, placards and flags
scattered across the cobblestones, boys on rooftops firing useless bullets at
the drab metal of the tanks.

He wondered if his sons had been foolish enough to waste their ammunition. At that moment, he was sure, they would be with others plotting a
counterattack; they were so earnest in their cause, faces enraptured when
they uttered the name of their goal. The last time they spoke, Drogic had
been tempted to ask them if they knew what freedom meant, yet knew that
would only drive the wedge deeper. When he had been their age, it had
been enough just to survive, just to drink a watery cabbage soup and find
a blanket to huddle in.

●

Inside the hotel room, he punched buttons of the remote control, exasperated that the TV broadcasts of four countries offered nothing but old
movies and gleeful contestants screaming for prizes. When news finally
did come on, it merely repeated the information in the papers. The leaders
of his rebellion were incensed at the invasion; the men who had sent the
tanks demanded capitulation; the city was quiet. Nothing but words. Film
crews hadn't delivered their pictures yet. More details to come on the late
reports.

●

Drogic surprised himself by sleeping. He woke up exhausted in the
morning, still wearing his traveling clothes. By now the screen showed the

rows of tanks flanking the square, more tanks lined up along the streets of the city, the shuttered windows, a few defiant banners, his native language inked across sheets hanging from rooftops, men in shirt sleeves and men in braided uniforms vehement before microphones, neither side willing to yield. A bulletin announced that the border was closed. Drogic could not return home until further notice. He spread his hands against the wall of his hotel room and pushed with all this strength, as if to hold back a torrent.

Then the phone rang and his meeting was canceled. The present instability made business decisions impossible. The man at the other end wished that all things would work out for the best and invited Drogic for an informal lunch at some time in the future, when things settled down.

•

Drogic thought to call his sister. He expected the lines to be jammed but got an immediate ringing. She lived with her family in the village of their youth, where his parents were buried. She was relieved to hear his voice but could tell him nothing; the state television station showed only the repeat of an old football match, the national team's most glorious victory. A thousand miles away he had much more information. How could she know about his sons?

Reaching his ex-wife in the city turned out to be very difficult. He had to dial again and again, met with busy signals or silence. "It's me," he said when she finally answered, and he could tell she was deciding how to react. Usually she just handed the phone to one of the boys or hung up with a curt "They're not here." But tonight she answered "Yes."

Drogic called her by name, and she burst into tears. "They haven't come home! I don't know where they are!"

"They're fine," he reassured her. "The news says people are staying off the streets. They probably went into a building when the trouble started."

"When will I see them?" she wept. Her misery annoyed him, this woman who had stood cursing while he packed to leave their apartment.

"When someone gives in," he told her, "when they work out a compromise." He hung up and imagined his sons, eyes gleaming, their grim young lips locked on the word "Never."

•

Drogic realized how hungry he was. He showered, changed clothes, and went down to the tables in the hotel garden. The day was brilliant and the city lush with flowers, thick beds of red and yellow blooming in the park across the street, shrubs spilling blossoms over the sidewalk. The city shone, spires of churches and palaces outlined against a vivid blue sky, shapes that he had loved for many years of visits. On both sides of a pedestrian street store windows sparkled with expensive treats. Despite his still damp hair and crisp clothes, Drogic felt soiled, as if he did not belong in this immaculate north.

•

A knot in his chest, Drogic ached to do something. He began striding toward his country's embassy, then stopped with the abrupt realization that the officials now in that building would hate someone like him; these were the people who welcomed the tanks.

With nothing but time, guilty at allowing himself his first day of leisure in months, he boarded a purple train that hugged the seacoast past tidy villages and harbors where sailboats drifted with the breeze. A country of ten thousand pleasures. It amazed him that people could lead such lives.

On a whim he got off the train at a station near the sea and walked to the beach, removing shoes and socks and standing in a business suit on the hard wet sand at the water's edge. Except for two mothers with babies, he was the only one there, staring out at the horizon, wondering if the women would consider him strange and report him to authorities. But when he turned toward them, they smiled and waved. He waved back.

Drogic recalled a beach not far from his city, on a small lake, not the sea, his sons just boys playing with toy guns, crouched behind clumps of weeds and firing noise bullets at strangers. When they shot at him, he seized his chest and toppled over, expecting them to run to his aid. But he had opened his eyes and found them circling warily, closing in for the kill.

That beach had been blighted by litter—broken bottles, rusting cans, torn newspapers skittering across the sand. His country could have been beautiful, but it was poor, mismanaged for decades, factories spewing a black haze, dumping chemical poison into the streams. Everything needed a coat of paint. Even the trees seemed faded.

•

In the village Drogic ate an expensive dinner and ordered a bottle of excellent wine. He lingered over the meal, alone at a table, savoring each taste as if he would never enjoy food again. He paid with a credit card, wondering whether he still had a bank account.

While he waited for his receipt, someone at the bar turned on a television set, and Drogic recognized the scene immediately. But now there were gunshots, the tank turrets swaying ominously, cars overturned and smoldering. In the background, half the city seemed in flames, radiant colors blazing across the large screen. Young men clung to weapons as they darted between barricades. One clutched an arm and looked at the camera in bewilderment, blood saturating his sleeve. Others appeared at the wounded man's side to rush him away. Then Drogic saw his first body, twisted on the cobblestones, legs splayed, feet naked in sandals, face turned into the gutter, a red stain spreading from his skull. He cried out and rose from his chair, reaching toward the set, then stopped when he realized a child was pointing at him, perplexed by his gesture.

•

At this time of the year so far north, night did not fall until very late. It amazed Drogic to look at his watch and see the sky bright at this hour. Nothing here was real. He rode a purple train back to the city of his hotel, rigid in his seat, with the sensation that he was being transported to a place he had never known, where he would be condemned to stay forever. He stared down at the veins on the back of his hand as if seeking a map that would guide him home.

•

Youngsters overwhelmed Drogic as he moved into the great waiting hall of the Central Station. Hordes of blond boys and girls surged from the local trains, hundreds of them, massed, arms linked, singing songs, flaunting laughter, cheering their team's victory, a great swell of youth spilling across the marble floor to the exit doors.

It was past midnight. Yawning, joints stiff from the rigid train seat, Drogic stood bewildered while the young people rushed past, certain he had entered a dream world of children.

He let the flow of youngsters sweep him up, push him along, across the wide street that separated the Central Station from the dazzling lights of an amusement park. He felt the intensity in their bodies, the force of their lives. They were oblivious of him, an unending young mass, blocking traffic, heedless of the blaring horns.

Drogic stopped to look at their faces and saw how beautiful they all were, eyes a brilliant blue, skin golden from the cool northern sun, features finely molded. Then he noticed the plastic bags of clinking amber beer bottles, the glass rims bought to their lips, their heads thrown back until foam ran down their chins. Drogic realized that these beautiful children were stumbling drunk. A slight girl tripped back against him, and he reached out to break her fall; but she staggered one step forward, clutched her middle, twisted her mouth, and spewed vomit. Her friends, boys and girls, faces radiant with laughter, circled around to carry her off as if nothing could spoil their pleasure.

One boy, not more than twelve, with a head of curls and wide brown eyes, looked back and smiled. Drogic squeezed fists, swallowing again and again until the children were gone.

•

His room dark but for the scenes of war on the television screen—tanks blasting, explosions, buildings ablaze, blood splattered on ancient walls—Drogic stood at the window and turned toward the spires of the city soaring in the twilight glow. He held himself ready to be moved by such beauty. But an anguish ripped through him like a live current and he twisted away. He would never see his sons again.

THE END OF THE CIRCLE

SHEILA NOTICED THE FAMILY FIRST. "Look!" The father knelt beside a baby boy propped against a door of the National Theatre on Karl Johans Gate, trying to place a carved troll in his small hands. She made George stop.

George paused to watch, eager to move on, humoring her, aware that babies were her weakness. She had given up teasing their own children to make her a grandmother, after he convinced her that it was useless, with two divorced and the third more interested in her career than motherhood.

George couldn't see the father's face, just the top of his tan scalp, balding in the manner of young men with fine blond hair. His muscular arms accentuated the thinness of the child's pale legs protruding from a padded diaper. The boy opened his fingers and watched the troll drop to the sidewalk. The father picked it up slowly, and this time wrapped the boy's arms around it so that he would hug it to his chest. Then the man let go and backed away. He pulled a videocam from the nylon bag slung over his shoulder and focused on the boy, puffing his cheeks and fluttering his lips to make him laugh. But the boy just stared. The man motioned his wife to get closer to the child.

George looked to the mother, a slight woman, fair and freckled, with loose red hair fanned by the breeze. She was peering across the street where a line of people queued at a bus stop, as if searching the faces. George followed her gaze, curious to know what she sought. "Julia!" the man called. But before she could move, the boy began to toddle toward his father, holding out the troll as if to return it. The man swept him up in a hug.

When he realized that George and Sheila were staring at them, he turned abruptly. From the flash of the man's grey eyes, George expected anger, insults, an embarrassing confrontation. The man's open shirt exposed a thin gold chain against his broad chest, and George swallowed at a sensation of danger. But the man broke into a smile and pointed at the videocam. "Would you mind taping the three of us?" he said, the accent plainly American. "All you have to do is look in the lens and press this button."

George laughed out loud. "I thought you were Norwegians."

He shook his head. "Oh no, we're apple pie and Fourth of July. Aren't we, Julia?"

"Upstate New York." Her voice rose, as if the fact startled her.

"What's your boy's name?" Sheila asked.

"Timothy." The father separated the syllables. "A big name for a little guy. And I'm called Ronny."

George, amused now, introduced himself and Sheila, said that they were delighted to be meeting Americans, though half the people they ran into at the hotels in Copenhagen and Stockholm had been from California. He expected Sheila's poke; she didn't like him chatting with strangers. Instead she reached out and touched fingertips to the boy's soft hair.

Ronny handed George the videocam and moved beside Julia at the National Theatre entrance, hoisted Timothy to his shoulders, and grinned at the lens. For a moment, the boy looked terrified to be so high. Then he reached down and blocked his father's nose with the troll's squat body, the gnarled wood rising like a growth between the man's eyes.

George thought it made a cute picture.

•

"He's too thin," Sheila said when they left the family.

"Who?"

"Timothy."

"Maybe he takes after Julia. She could use a few pounds herself."

"He's nothing like her."

George realized that the boy was dark, different from both parents— black hair, large brown eyes with long, thick lashes. "Then he's probably a finicky eater, the way Greg was at his age. Now look at our son."

"Greg was never that scrawny," she insisted.

Though he wanted to say, what is it to you, George took her hand, unwilling to let her anxiety ruin his mood. He was feeling happy, strolling on a wide promenade of under a brilliant sky.

"What a pleasant city Oslo is," he said. They moved onto a shaded path beside a circular fountain that sprayed a cool mist. George nodded at three elderly women on a bench eating ice cream. They saluted with their cones.

•

Later, when they crossed the road from the City Hall to the fjord, George saw the family sitting at an outdoor cafe on the water's edge. Ronny called out to them, lifted Timothy to his lap, and gestured at the two empty chairs.

"Why not?" George said. He found himself eager for company, a diversion from the weeks of sightseeing. He gave Sheila a quick glance and guided her forward with a hand on her shoulder.

Ronny signaled the waiter and pointed to the sizzling plates of grilled shrimp at the next table. "That's what we're having."

George nodded. "Sounds great."

Julia's blue eyes gazed out across the fjord, but George saw only the glints of sunlight on the water. Sheila asked if she could hold Timothy, and Ronny passed the boy to her. In her arms he squirmed for a few seconds, whimpered once, and then lay still, face pressed into her shoulder. She brushed the top of his head with her lips. About to tell her to stop, it's not yours, George saw the urgency in her face and kept silent, uneasy at his own annoyance. He wondered if the others noticed. Her need bewildered him. They'd already raised a family.

When she returned the boy to his father, George looked away to study the rigging of a sailing ship moored at pier beside the cafe. Beyond it a fortress rose on a bluff that overlooked the fjord.

Ronny pointed at the stone walls. "What do Norwegians have to be afraid of?" Timothy sat on his lap and sucked juice from a bottle.

"Swedes once. Germans in the 20th century." Though Ronny's words had been teasing, Julia spoke with a gravity that surprised George. "It's called the Akershus Fortress, and the Nazis shot Resistance fighters there. After the war, it's where Quisling was executed."

Ronny sliced the edge of his hand across his throat and made a squishing sound. "Doesn't pay to be a traitor."

"How do you know so much?" Sheila asked Julia, almost an accusation.

"I read."

George found himself drawn toward her. Despite her ethereal look, Julia was a direct young woman, grieving over events that had taken place decades ago, long before she was born, back when he and Sheila were Timothy's age. Though he barely knew them, he had trouble matching her with Ronny, she so frail and serious, he so solid and breezy.

The waiter brought the plates of shrimp and, at Ronny's signal, another round of beers. A passenger ferry left its slip, churning a wake as it moved toward an arm of green land across the water. "Museums are over there." Julia pointed. "The Kon Tiki and the Viking ship."

"We should hire you as a guide," Sheila said. "How long have you been here?" George had been about to ask the same question.

"In Norway just days. In Europe three months."

George sighed, an exaggerated sound of regret. "I wish we could have done that at your age. We didn't make our first trip till we were forty. Couldn't afford it before."

"Neither can we." Ronny winked.

"But you're here," Sheila said.

"Ronny's between jobs." Julia leaned forward to dab Timothy's mouth with her napkin.

"Cleaned out all our savings. Poof." Ronny exploded his hands. "Bone dry. Five credit cards up to their limit."

George nodded, surprised that Julia would let him be so irresponsible. "Then what?" he asked. "When will you go back?"

"There's so much we haven't seen." Julia spoke quickly, as if to insert herself before Ronny could answer.

"I'm taking my son on the Grand Tour." He bounced Timothy on his knee, and the boy squeezed his eyes shut at the rough ride.

•

Although Ronny reached for his wallet, George insisted on paying for the meal, conscious that he had so much, eager to treat people living out what had once been his fantasy.

They crossed the road together and stood in awkward silence by the blank red brick of the City Hall, George glancing at Julia, hoping she would speak, trying to think of a way to continue the encounter, when Sheila asked, "What are your plans for the afternoon?" George was surprised that she too wanted to be with them, then understood that it was the child. He awaited their response, suddenly concerned that Ronny and Julia wouldn't want to waste the day with an aged couple.

"The Vigeland sculptures," Julia said.

"Us too," George said quickly.

"They're supposed to be a highlight." Ronny's face brightened. "Why don't we go together?"

George signaled for a cab and folded the stroller into the trunk while Ronny held Timothy. As soon as they set off, Ronny insisted on paying this time, slipping a crisp 100 kroner note from his wallet and rolling it into a tight tube as the driver maneuvered through the streets.

•

In Frogner Park, sunbathers sprawled on towels spread over the rolling grass, young people mainly, the women casually topless. For an instant George expected a comment from Ronny, a joking allusion to Julia's thin chest. But all the man did was throw his arms to the sky and say, "What a day!" George wondered how he could have had such a notion.

The first of the sculptures, bronze figures of men and women and infants, rose on columns from a bridge, then ahead large white shapes sat in a circle around a monolith. "The Wheel of Life," Julia told them.

When George got close, he realized the statues captured the cycle of human existence—mothers with babies, frolicking children, couples, families, friendships, finally old age and the moments before death. Though the figures were thick stone, almost crudely hewn, the faces indistinct, George found himself moved, struck by how close he and Sheila were to the end of the cycle. If the five of them made a circle in age from Timothy to himself, they could form their own wheel.

"I don't like this," Julia pointed at the monolith. Though it towered above the individual statues, George had not given it close attention. Now he recognized a mass of human forms, limbs linked, piled one atop the other.

"It's supposed to show the continuum of humanity," Julia said, "but it reminds me of concentration camps." She did not look away.

George nodded, made uneasy by the tangle of bodies. He turned to Sheila for a reaction, but she was watching Timothy. When Ronny seated him atop a stone child and stepped back to tape, she moved close, as if to protect the boy from a fall. Ronny swung the videocam toward Julia and George by the monolith, focusing on them so long their smiles froze.

•

Standing next to Julia beneath sweeping green tree limbs, Sheila on a path helping Ronny lift Timothy into his stroller, George had an impulse to invite them to spend time with them, to share the cabin they had rented for a week on a farm in the hills above Lillehammer. He knew he should have consulted Sheila but hoped she wouldn't resent an opportunity to spend time with the boy. For him, it was Julia's quiet appeal, his sense that something very deep ran inside her. He cleared his throat and asked.

When Julia turned to Sheila to say they couldn't impose, George had a moment of panic, unsure what his wife would do. But when Sheila gave a faint smile, he relaxed and explained that the cabin had two bedrooms and that there would be plenty of space. He saw Ronny signal Julia and step in front of her. "All right. But we'll pay half."

"It's already paid for," George argued, "in advance. And it wouldn't cost us any less if you weren't there."

"Then you'll have to let us buy the groceries." Ronny shook his hand as if they were sealing a deal.

•

All evening George kept waiting for Sheila to speak about it, but she said nothing beyond commenting on the food at dinner and telling him how tired she felt. But she was still reading her book when he turned out the light on his side of the bed and rolled over.

Early the next morning, when they went down to their hotel lobby, George found the family waiting. Timothy was sleeping on a padded chair, mouth open, dried mucus clogging his nostrils. Julia had on the same flowered dress and Ronny the same blue shirt they had worn the previous day, his chain flashing in the artificial light.

George's plan was for them all to take a cab to Fornebu Airport, where he had reserved a Hertz Volvo, a station wagon with room for six. But

Ronny cleared his throat. "We don't have all our stuff with us now." He and Julia carried only two small zippered bags

Sheila brushed a hand over the matched luggage set she and George had aligned on the lobby carpet. "Where is it?"

"At the Central Station. In a locker."

"We thought the car rental was there," Julia said.

Sheila shook her head. "No, only at the airport."

"You all wait here," George said. "There's no sense in everybody going."

"I'll come with you," Ronny insisted. He rode with George in the taxi, apologizing several times for messing up their plans despite George's protests that it didn't matter, that they were on vacation and had open days ahead. "We've been taking public transportation for so long," Ronny explained, "that we've forgotten what it's like with a car."

Once they had the station wagon, George decided to retrieve the family's luggage before returning to the hotel for Sheila, Julia, and Timothy. "Then they can just pile in and we'll drive north." He hoped Sheila would soften toward Julia while the two of them were alone.

Ronny's key wouldn't turn in the oversized locker no matter how hard he twisted. George put on reading glasses to study the lock and saw that more coins were needed; he reached into his pocket and dropped several kroner into the slot while Ronny watched.

Ronny swung open the locker door and gripped the frame of a backpack, sliding it out and then bracing it on the floor before he hoisted it onto his shoulders. Thick rolls of nylon—bright yellow and blue—were strapped to both sides, two pairs of hiking boots tied to the bottom by their laces.

George slid a hand over the slick material. "What's this for?"

"A tent. Poles inside the pack. Sleeping out gets you close to nature. Saves money too."

"Last night?"

"No. We pooled pennies and found a room."

"How long can you keep this up?"

"As long as I have to."

George expected Ronny's deep laugh, as if he had made a joke, but the man stared ahead.

•

Route E6 north narrowed to two lanes a few miles above the city. Everyone rode with headlights on despite the brightness of the day. Julia explained that it was the law in the Scandinavian countries. "And they do obey the law here," Ronny said. "Never drink and drive, George. You'll spend the rest of your life in a Norwegian clink." His tone was teasing, but George sensed an edge of mockery.

"I'm grateful for the warning," he said. He tried to watch the scenery as he drove, the rolling green of the countryside, the glimpses of Lake Mjosa through the thick trees, but his eyes were drawn to the mirror where he could see Julia gripping an arm rest and Ronny hugging Timothy on his lap, smacking kisses on his forehead while the boy reached up to touch his father's unshaven jaw. Sheila reached back and stroked Timothy's cheek, mimicking his gesture.

"Is he always so good?" she asked.

"Timothy is a wonder." Ronny squeezed his son tight with a loud ooomph. Then he put on a stern face. "Don't you ever misbehave, boy. I don't want to lose you in a Norwegian jail."

Julia stared straight ahead as if mesmerized by the rhythm of the ride. When she sensed George watching her reflection, she forced a smile. Timothy closed a fist around his father's gold chain and tugged.

•

A dog began barking and leaping at its tether when George parked the Volvo outside the farmhouse. They had been twisting upward on a narrow road for fifteen minutes, ears popping as they climbed higher and higher. Timothy pressed fingers into his, mouth contorted as if he were about to cry. Ronny made calming sounds the whole time.

Mrs. Sundt, the farmer's wife, had limited English, memorized phrases about the electricity and the microwave, a few pleasantries. George saw that she seemed startled by the appearance of the family with them, seeking words to express her bewilderment.

"These are new friends," George tried to explain, speaking very slowly.

"Jegg er venn." Julia read from her phrasebook, pointing to herself and then to Sheila and George.

"Ja. Ja." Mrs. Sundt furrowed her brow as if unconvinced while she led them up a path to a shingled cabin.

"It's perfect," George said when the woman unlocked the door and showed them inside, all lacquered white pine, walls, ceiling, and floor, the furniture pine, everything smelling fresh and new.

He and Ronny unloaded the station wagon and carried the luggage and the backpack to the bedrooms. After she and George arranged their clothing on the built-in shelves, Sheila volunteered to do the shopping in the village market at the bottom of the hill because George wouldn't know what to buy. Julia offered to help and motioned Ronny to slip her some cash. But he made a show of passing it to her, fluttering the bills from his fingertips.

When Sheila and Julia left, Ronny put Timothy down for a nap and opened the empty refrigerator. "I wish we had some beer."

"Now that they can't arrest us," George said.

"You never can tell when they'll come and get you." "

"Not in Norway," George joked.

"You always have to watch your back."

They moved outside to take in the view from the front porch. A tin-roofed barn filled the foreground. George couldn't see any cattle but heard them lowing in their stalls. A blue tractor sat parked in a field of new sprouts. Across a wide still river dark green pines grew up the hillsides. The river twisted under a bridge and then disappeared behind a bend in the landscape. Thin layers of white clouds hung unmoving high in the sky.

"I could stay here forever." Ronny stretched both arms upwards and sighed.

"Have you considered living in Europe?" George asked him.

"Oh, I've considered everything."

"What does Julia say?"

"Julia, you may have noticed, is big on information, but not solutions."

"You're lucky in your wife," he said, resenting the tone of Ronny's voice. "Julia is very pleasant."

"More so when we started out. All this traveling hasn't done much for her disposition."

"Then why do you go on?"

"We do what we have to do."

George gave him a puzzled look, but Ronny's eyes were closed, his head tilted back in the chair as if he, like his son, were already asleep. George couldn't decide if his large, full features were handsome; they should have been, but something was a little off, not quite centered.

•

Sheila and Julia came up with sacks of groceries. They took turns showing off their purchases, one at a time, pleased with their choices. George smiled back at them both, glad that they were getting on so well, relieved at his wife's good mood.

"Wine. Bordeaux." Sheila held up two bottles. "Julia and Ronny's treat."

"Orange juice." Julia pulled out the container. "Milk for Timothy."

"Salad."

"Fresh fish."

"A feast," George said. "Who needs restaurants?"

Ronny came in from the porch, rubbing his eyes. "Let me do the preparations."

"Can he cook?" Sheila teased Julia.

"When he wants to," Julia said. "It's one of his talents."

"And what are the others?"

"Those," Ronny winked, "are confidential."

•

They ate at a picnic table at the side of the cottage, using juice glasses for the wine. Both Sheila and George praised Ronny's cooking and told him he should make a career as a chef, though George didn't really believe he was quite that good. But the food, the Bordeaux, and the long northern evening had made him expansive.

They exchanged tales of places they had visited, Julia and Ronny in recent weeks, Sheila and George over many years. Mountains, lakes, villages, cities. Wonderful experiences to share, George thought, delighting in his memories.

When the wine was gone, Ronny held an empty bottle in each hand and shook both over his glass. "Dead soldiers. Time for the aquavit."

George saw Julia clutch at his knee under the table when he stood up to enter the cabin.

Back in seconds, standing over the others, Ronny poured the clear liquor into their wineglasses, Julia's turning pink from the leftover wine. Then he toasted. "Skol!" Sheila sipped and made a face. George sputtered when he tasted. "My God! This is strong." Ronny threw his head back and drained his, then gave an openmouthed sigh. "Another of my talents." He poured for himself again. Julia just swished her glass.

Timothy was playing on the grass, eyeing a grey cat at the edge of the crops, child and animal staring at each other, the cat darting away each time the boy lunged toward it. Near 11, when the darkness thickened, Ronny sprang from the table and swept up his son. "Time for beddy bye." The boy began shrieking, face suddenly red, mouth a wide circle. "Look who's having a tantrum," Ronny chanted.

"I'm so sorry." Julia apologized, her pale cheeks flushed.

"Don't be silly." Sheila said. "I raised three just like him. They do grow out of it. Eventually."

George said he would clean up and do the dishes. "You both take care of poor Timothy. Soothe his miseries."

Before he moved toward the bedroom, Ronny reached back for the aquavit, the bottle dangling from his fingertips as the boy thrashed against him. Julia hesitated in the hallway, then followed them inside and closed the door.

•

In bed, George cleared his throat, tried to speak softly. "Is this all right?"

"The boy. Timothy. He's not a happy child." "The way his father dotes on him?"

"How often does he laugh?"

George realized she was right. "Is it important?"

"Were our children like that?"

"But she's fine," he said, hesitant. "I really like her."

"Can't you see how edgy she is?" Sheila spoke in a harsh whisper. "I can feel her nerves vibrating."

After a silence, he made himself ask, "Did I make a mistake?" Sheila twisted her head into the pillow and turned toward to sleep.

•

A sudden noise made them both sit up with a start. It was pitch black, the middle of the night. A thumping resounded from the other bedroom, at first a steady rhythm, then frenzied, stopping abruptly with a loud twang of bedsprings.

"My God!" Sheila said. "The child's with them."

"It's probably not the first time. They sleep in a tent."

"I expected better from her."

When the silence continued, they relaxed and pulled up the covers. George could tell Sheila was furious, but he decided not to speak of his own disappointment, not then, maybe some time in the future. He lay awake remembering the first years of their own marriage—passion in a car, under a tree, but never in front of the children, never as houseguests. He imagined Julia pinned under Ronny's thick body, his eyes squeezed shut, throat taut, mouth clenched, while she stared up at the darkness.

Later, from her breathing George could tell that Sheila had fallen asleep again. He had to use the toilet and tiptoed barefoot on the cool wooden floor, closing the door slowly, trying to muffle his sounds, hesitant to lift the plunger and disturb the cottage with the surge of flushing.

When the noise died, he stepped out to the living room and saw the door to the porch open, Julia at the railing outlined in the first glow of dawn, wearing a long nightgown, shivering in the chill.

George moved beside her. "Are you all right?"

He could see her tears when she turned to him. He touched her shoulder and she fell against him, shaking with sobs. He closed his arms around her, feeling the ridge of her spine, the ribs under her taut skin. There was nothing to her.

"We didn't do anything," she wept. "It wasn't sex. There hasn't been any sex in weeks."

"What then?"

"Ronny jumping up and down on the mattress, getting wilder and wilder."

"Was he drunk?"

"Ronny does crazy things. Everything's fine, and then he snaps."

"But why?"

"It's the way we live." Her body wrenched in a spasm, shuddering in his arms.

George stoked her hair, wondering what would happen if he kissed her. It startled him that he wanted to kiss her, that he had so misunderstood the nature of his affection. As he pulled her closer, he heard the click of a door lock and sensed Ronny's eyes staring out at them from the dark cabin.

He eased his embrace but could not release her. "What can I do?"

She touched his face with a fingertip. "You're a nice man. You have a nice wife. You shouldn't worry about strangers." She pulled away and disappeared inside.

•

George finally dozed toward morning, and it seemed only minutes later that Sheila was shaking his arm. "Let's go for a walk," she said. "I need fresh air."

He needed coffee first, brewing the water while she dressed, then sitting on the couch with the hot cup listening for sounds from the other bedroom; but even Timothy was quiet. He wondered if Julia were awake too, as he had been, unable to sleep, lying rigidly with her arms fixed at her sides.

Out on the path behind the farm, they saw Mr. Sundt carrying great brown sacks from a shed to the barn. George repeated what Julia had told him.

"Why should he want to do that to us?"

He placed a hand on Sheila's shoulder to calm her. "There's something going on between them. We don't have anything to do with it. You were right. I hadn't realized how unhappy she is."

"I'm not overjoyed myself. This is supposed to be our vacation."

"We used to fight once. Remember?"

"Of course I do," she said. "And we were poor once. And we raised three children. And we're still putting up with the aftershock of two divorces."

"But you and me—we're ok."

"We're the best we can be, George." He wouldn't ask her what she meant.

•

When they got back to the cabin, Julia was in the shower. Water beat against the metal stall. Ronny fixed breakfast for his son, the boy naked beneath an undershirt, swollen belly and gaunt thighs. George could smell the diaper in the plastic garbage pail.

"I'll get rid of it," Ronny's tone was annoyed though neither one of them had complained.

"It's all right," George said. He had come in half expecting the man to curse him for embracing his wife, rise up and smash a fist into his soft middle. When nothing happened, he feared that Sheila would abuse Ronny for his deception.

"We had plans to go to a national park today," she said instead. "Rondale, up in the mountains. It may be too long a ride for Timothy."

"We'll go with you." Ronny spoke abruptly, surly. "There's nothing to do here. You don't know what it's like spending months trying to figure out how to fill the day."

"You've had all of Europe."

"Well, when you come down to it, Europe is just a place like any other."

George hadn't heard Julia enter the kitchen, looked up with surprise to see her standing there in jeans and a tee shirt, her damp red hair pulled back in a knot, accentuating the sharp bones of her face. She met his eyes. "Maybe you and Sheila would like to be by yourselves."

"No. That's all right." He didn't want to leave her alone with Ronny.

•

On the E6 at Ringebu, George saw signs pointing right for the stave church; but he didn't tell the others, unwilling to make a stop and go through the bother of tourist conversation. They all rode without speaking, the only sounds Timothy's whines as he twisted on his father's lap. Ronny kept shifting the boy's position to make him comfortable. In the mirror, he could see the man grit his teeth. Sheila was smoldering too, he

knew, in another way, furious at him for offering no way out of this situation. George tensed himself, wondering what would happen if he reached
over and shook her, demanded: what do you want me to do? make them
get out on the side of the road? But he clutched the wheel and said nothing.

Ronny was the one who broke the silence, snapping at the boy. "God-
damnit, Timothy. Stop fidgeting!"

Julia reached out. "Here. Let me hold him for a while."

"You? What good are you?"

Sheila turned in sudden anger. "She's his mother!"

Ronny poked Julia's shoulder, again and again, until she drew away
from him. "Hear that. The lady thinks you're his mother."

Sheila glared at him. "Your wife then." Forced laughter rasped at his
throat.

"I'm nothing." Julia closed both fists in her hair and pulled it loose,
twisting it under her chin. "I'm not a mother and I'm not a wife."

Although she spoke quietly, George found himself roaring. "Just shut
up! Everybody just shut up!"

Timothy began wailing. When Ronny ignored him, folded arms and
stared out the window, Julia lifted the boy onto her lap and pulled him
against her thin chest.

●

George considered turning around, then knew it wouldn't be any better at the cabin. So he drove ahead, following signs, turning onto a
narrow, pitted road of sharp curves through the rock. He saw few buildings, rare signs of human life, as the car climbed through miles of dense
stunted pines. In the back seat, Julia pressed her face into Timothy's hair,
eyes shut, tears squeezed from beneath the lashes. Ronny clenched both
fists, the veins of his arms bulging, a sharp pulse in the tendons of his neck.

George missed the turn to the park, an arrow outside a brown building
pointing up a long dirt path gouged with tire tracks. He slammed into
reverse, clashed gears, then swerved forward.

The landscape was desolate, the ground nothing but rock and lichen,
dust swirling across the windshield, dark snow-streaked peaks in the distance.

The road pitched them back and forth, deep ruts jarring them off their seats. George refused to slow down until heavy chains blocked the road ahead. He had to stop in a parking area among a few scattered cars and two large tour buses. They couldn't go any further.

"Who on earth would want to come here?" George said aloud, hoping they all could be tourists again. But no one answered him.

He opened the station wagon door to step out onto a path, but was stunned by a fierce, chill wind. He wasn't wearing a jacket; none of them were. He slammed the door shut. "It's freezing out there."

"Timothy does have a mother, and Ronny does have a wife," Julia said, as if to no one, and hugged the child tighter. "But it's not me."

"Maybe an ex-wife." Ronny sneered. "We left town before the divorce was final."

"Something's wrong, isn't it?" Sheila said. "You shouldn't be here."

Julia nodded. "We ran off before she got custody. And now we're afraid to go home."

"Did you love him so much?" Sheila asked.

"I did. I loved him desperately."

George wanted to shout: Stop talking! I don't want to hear!

"You can't go on this way." Sheila spoke calmly, very slowly.

"Ronny won't admit it."

"Goddamn you!" Ronny swung toward Julia to rip Timothy from her. She locked the boy between her knees and slapped at him.

"Hey!" George turned and groped behind to separate them, Julia's swats stinging his arms, Ronny's fists pounding his shoulder. Julia twisted away and forced the boy between the front seats to Sheila. Then she dropped her hands to her sides, defenseless, waiting for Ronny's blows. The man was livid, face bloated with rage.

He'll kill her, George thought, tensed, ready to hurl himself into the back of the station wagon. Instead Ronny threw open the door and shouted at Sheila: "Keep the brat! I'm sick of him!" He tumbled out onto the gravel, trying to run down the road past the chain barrier. The force of wind knocked him backward. He crouched, covered his face with his hands, and plunged ahead, punching and clawing at the air. Hail began to fall, large pellets suddenly bouncing off the earth, clanging at the steel roof of the Volvo.

"Should I go after him?" George asked Julia.

"He'll come back. He always does."

"What next then?"

Her eyes were hollow, her lips so pinched she seemed to have no mouth. "Get rid of us. Get us out of your lives."

Timothy was wailing. Sheila held him close and began to rock, singing softly, his screams obliterating her soothing. George sensed that this child would never stop shrieking. He would shriek even when he was silent. And George wished he could flee, but his limbs felt like stone.

SOMEONE ELSE

"You're traveling alone, aren't you?" she said.

Mark nodded at the large young woman standing over him in the train aisle, then turned back to watch people move in and out of the station. He hoped that was the end of it and she would go away. But she dropped her backpack and sat on the seat facing his. He pretended to be intent on searching the crowd, as if expecting someone. The woman's image reflected in the window of the coach, flat and transparent, a double exposure over the great mountains surrounding the town.

"Look at them all running around like idiots." She gestured with an abrupt sweep of her hand.

"Who?" Mark followed her pointing to see if she had noticed something unusual, but nothing seemed to have changed, just people hurrying with luggage and knapsacks.

"Like they're desperate to get to someplace." Despite the insistence of her words, her voice was toneless, a straight line on a graph.

"Travel can make people anxious." He was sorry he had spoken.

"Then they ought to stay home. Travel should be special. Without schedules or plans or limits. Absolutely free. The way it is for you."

His head snapped in surprise and he looked at her full face for the first time. "What makes you think that?"

She pointed at his pack in the overhead rack, then down at his boots, new for this trip, hardly worn. "When you're by yourself, you can go anywhere you want."

"Is that what you do?"

She grinned, knobby teeth in a wide mouth. "It's amazing how free a person can be."

•

She'd done it. Despite Mark's resolution to ignore her, she'd trapped him into a conversation. Instead of gazing out at the mountains for the next two hours, he'd have to endure the slow, flat drone of her monologue, her bland round face blocking every view.

Mark cringed at the memory of his first reaction to her, when in the station he had seen the long tanned legs stretched from a waiting room bench, the bare shoulders. She had been leaning over to study a map, face obscured by a flap of paper, and he had a quick fantasy of a traveling partner, alone in a compartment, running his hands up those long legs. Then she stood and stretched, an ungainly round-shouldered woman in a brown sleeveless top and skimpy pink running shorts, her legs shapeless as logs. He had burned with humiliation, as if everyone in the tourist-jammed room had read his thoughts and knew what a fool he was.

•

The train started to move toward the great mountains, a line of narrow red cars, creaking slowly in the square across from the station. This town was a major junction, a hub to destinations all over the continent, hundreds of possibilities. And now, the woman facing him, he felt certain he had made the worst possible choice.

"Why here?" she asked.

"What do you mean?"

"Of all the places to be in the world, why are you here now?"

Mark wouldn't tell her that he had abandoned his friend Freddy when Freddy got Linda's call, determined to stick to the route they had planned, certain it would be far from any destination that Linda would want. "Same reason as you, I suppose?"

"How do you know my reason?"

"To see one of the world's most famous views. A mountain in a million."

"That's not why."

He wouldn't give her the satisfaction of asking, didn't care what made her want to do anything, certain that despite her pose she was just another gawking tourist. A mountain in a million: those had been Freddy's words. Damn Freddy. Damn Linda. Damn them both. If Linda hadn't decided to be contrite, he wouldn't be sitting here having to put up with this woman.

Mark had planned this European trip for Freddy's sake, to divert his friend after Linda broke their engagement. In a restaurant, the night after she returned the ring, it had disturbed Mark to see such a big man suddenly bury his face in his hands, shoulders heaving, tears beading in the hair of his knuckles. Feeling the stares from the other tables, Mark had squirmed on his chair as if the shame were his.

He had tried to plead Freddy's case with Linda, sitting beside her on her sofa, and describing the man's misery. "But I don't love him," Linda had said, at first calmly, shaking her head, as if discussing a book she didn't like, and then—when Mark kept insisting that she must —repeated the words louder and louder until she was hysterical, pounding her fists on his chest. He had grabbed her wrists, wrapped his arms around her to stop her fury, and found himself kissing her, body thrashing in sudden passion while his mind chilled with dread. He had wrenched himself free and slammed the door, twisting sleepless through the night, unable to convince himself what happened was an accident, reliving each second to determine if she had responded, if it had only been him. The next evening, when he handed Freddy a stack of travel brochures, he couldn't look his friend in the face. He chattered about awesome views and hoped neither of them would ever see Linda again.

But yesterday she had called their hotel in Zurich in the middle of the first night after their arrival, confusing the time shift, thinking Europe was six hours earlier. Mark had answered, jetlagged, clutching the phone and moaning "Yes." He recognized her immediately just from the sound of her tentative "Freddy?" He dropped the phone and shook his friend awake, angry, knowing the trip would be ruined, certain that Linda—suddenly remorseful—was about to announce that she was flying over the next day. Freddy, manic with joy, swirled Mark in a bear hug.

Linda wanted cities, not mountain trails, and Freddy had spent the hours till dawn revising the itinerary, talking nonstop, oblivious as Mark wadded clothes into his pack. When he saw Mark standing at the door, he protested, invited him to go with them, sure Linda wouldn't mind. She really liked Mark. "No, she doesn't," Mark said and, for a moment, wondered if she were actually coming to see him. He checked out before the breakfast room opened, eager to get away from the two of them.

•

"What do people call you?" the woman asked, her legs crossed, worn Birkenstocks dangling from the ends of her toes.

"They call me Mark."

"Like German money. *Geld*."

"I'm not sure of my exchange value," he said, surprising himself with the comment.

She laughed, an openmouthed intake of breath, then paused waiting for him to say more. He wouldn't ask her name in return, hoping she wouldn't offer it, as if knowing would somehow connect him with her; but anonymity would erase their conversation the moment the train reached its destination.

"You're a walker, aren't you, Mark?" she said.

He shook his head. "A runner."

"The mountains aren't a good place for running."

"I just got here. I haven't tried."

"I've been walking for months, everywhere," she said. "I only take trains for long distances."

"I didn't plan to run."

"That's smart, Mark .I twisted my knee running down a trail. Tore some cartilage, I think."

He looked down at her crossed legs expecting to see swelling, but both knees appeared the same above the shapeless calves. "When was this?"

"A few weeks ago. On the islands."

"Islands? In this country?"

"In the Aegean." "Doing what?"

"Fleeing from a shepherd."

For an instant Mark thought he was supposed to laugh but saw the grim set of her face, swallowed a sigh, and leaned back to hear her tale.

•

"It's different for a man. Traveling alone. In some places, lots of places, men think a woman traveling by herself is easy." She paused as if waiting for him to comment. "Usually people ask me why I do it. And I tell them I can take care of myself, see things they'll never see shuffling around with a group. So I haggled for a seat on a mail boat and ended up on this island where tourists never go. It isn't on most maps. They didn't even have an inn. Nobody speaks English. I used hand gestures to arrange a room with a family. I had the beach to myself. Everybody else was out in fishing boats or tending sheep. I'd just take a book and lie in the sun. That's why I'm so tan now." She rubbed a palm over her thigh. "There was this one shepherd I'd see every day with his goats on the path to the beach. A skinny little man with a beard like steel wool. I tried smiling and saying hello, but he just stared as if I'd just landed from outer space. So one morning after I'd been there a couple of weeks I'm lying between two dunes with my top off and I hear a step in the sand. Before I could even sit up, this shepherd leaps out from behind a rock shouting something in Greek. And he grabs my boobs. Just like that."

She held two cupped hands over her brown top, and for an instant Mark thought she was going to seize herself. But both hands clenched into fists.

"The bastard squeezed," she said, angry now, face flushed, "like he was milking goats. I tried to kick him where it would really hurt, but I just put my foot in his gut. He fell backwards and that gave me enough time to grab my pack and start swinging out at him. Still he came after me. I ran off the beach with him right on my heels, me screaming and hitting him with the pack. He kept tripping and picking himself up again. The son of a bitch wouldn't stop."

"So what happened?" Mark asked, wondering if she were making up the story, unable to imagine any man driven wild with lust for her, remembering how his hand burned on Linda's breast before he tore himself away.

"Somebody came. People. A family. And he turned and fled. I'm standing there waving my arms and shouting, forgetting that I'm topless and wondering why those people and their kids are gawking at me like that."

"Weren't you scared?"

She shook her head. "Just pissed off. He was pathetic."

Mark pictured her fighting the shepherd, a filthy man with a wild dark beard, certain that she had been too foolish to recognize the danger she was in. He imagined himself deep in shadow on an isolated trail and wondered if he would be as vulnerable in these mountains—a man alone.

•

For the rest of the trip Mark stole glances out at crags and peaks, the stands of pines near the tracks and the ice caps above the tree line, regretting all that he was missing. The woman droned on with tales of her travels, like displaying snapshots of a hundred anonymous scenes. It struck him that for all the places she had been she just blathered trivial de-tails— breaking in boots in Montalcino, doing laundry in Avignon, leaving her passport at the hotel in Llubljana, cashing a check in Brindisi. It was as if she had no memories of cities or landscapes, as if for all her claims of discovery she experienced nothing but petty annoyances. Even now, spectacular views around every bend, she focused on him and jabbered.

Just before their station, where the line ended, they passed through a tunnel, and, for a second, in a sudden blackness before the lights flashed back on, Mark thought her leg pressed his. But as the glare returned, he blinked and saw her calf at least eight inches away.

When the train halted and they stood, he realized she was his height and probably weighed as much with her broad back and thick limbs, strong enough to break that shepherd's neck. He lifted her pack from the seat so that she could slip arms through the straps. It was bulging and heavy, something metallic clanging in the front pouch.

An elderly couple nodded and let them into the line of debarking pas-sengers, she first and he directly behind. They stood side by side on the platform.

"What are you going to do now, Mark?" she asked. He shrugged.

"Get my bearings, I guess."

"I need a cold drink," she said.

"I'm not thirsty." He set his pack on a bench, pretending to search through a pocket. She took a few steps and paused to look back.

"Enjoy the rest of your trip," he told her.

She walked toward the station building and all he could see of her were two legs beneath the hump of her backpack.

Mark adjusted buckles until sure that she was a distance away, re-lieved to be by himself on the platform. For a moment, he felt guilty, as if it were wrong to abandon her, such a lonely woman. All she'd wanted to do was talk. But then he'd never be able to get rid of her. She'd probably already trapped another stranger in the waiting room anyway.

By the track across from him a man and woman embraced, and he imagined them as Freddy and Linda, her hands clutching at Freddy's face as they had for a second clutched at his. Had it been to push him away or pull him closer? Mistaken identity, he muttered half aloud and thought that was true for all of them—Linda, Freddy, the woman on the train, the passionate shepherd, himself. All grabbing at strangers in desperate need.

·

Even though he was hungry and the village filled with tourist restaurants, Mark wouldn't stop, unsure which she had chosen for her cold drink. He bought rolls at a bakery and chewed them as he threaded through the crowded streets, swallowing wads of tough dough, eager to get away, to rise far up into the mountains.

Arrows pointed toward the cableway, an uphill walk to the other edge of the village. Mark passed rows of hotels, shop windows displaying expensive watches and cashmere sweaters. Electric carts whined alongside him on the narrow auto-less road. A pack of adolescent girls had fallen in behind him, all very blonde, chattering in a singsong language he couldn't identify. They began to whisper and break out in shrill giggles. Mark was sure they were talking about him, but when he stopped and wheeled abruptly, they looked past him and turned into a side street.

The cable car was the size of a hotel room. He had a fifteen-minute wait before the next ascent, and as people boarded and filled the space against the windows, he noticed he was the only one without skis. The rest wore stretch pants and unsnapped boots of thick bright plastic. Dark glasses and goggles covered their eyes.

By the time the car began its climb, it was packed, Mark pressed against the side clinging to a handgrip. Most of the people were speaking German or Italian. When they lifted above the trees, the famous view spread out before him, the mountain in a million, directly above but fogged by the scratched plastic window.

Behind him Mark heard a conversation in English, two young American males hovering over a woman in tight red pants, her back toward him. He stood admiring the shape of her when she turned to smile up at one of the men. Linda. It was Linda. Even though she wore wraparound sunglasses, he was certain of it. Mark leaned forward, blocked by three tall Germans, scanning the car for Freddy. He wanted to shout out to her but couldn't make himself speak, uncertain what was happening, what he was seeing, afraid to call attention to himself.

The car thumped over a joint in the cable, and one of the Germans said something, making his friends laugh. The two Americans were listening closely to the woman, to Linda, as if she were telling them something very important. But Mark couldn't hear. There were too many people, too many voices. He tried to edge around the Germans to move closer to her but their skis blocked him in.

With an abrupt jolt, the car ended its climb at a midpoint. By the time Mark stepped out onto the platform, she was far ahead in the tunnel to the small gondolas that completed the journey to the mountaintop, the two Americans nowhere in sight.

Mark hurried after her, threading his way through the others, just ten yards behind as she was about to enter a gondola. This time he called out. "Linda!" And she turned toward the sound, smiled at his gesture, his outstretched arm, but stepped inside and closed the door. He wasn't sure, couldn't see her now. If it wasn't Linda, it was her double, a person very much like her. But how could Linda have abandoned Freddy? What if she had come to find him, if she wanted him to follow? It couldn't be so, Mark told himself. The woman had to be someone else.

When the gondola lifted, he went back into the tunnel, past the locked ski racks, and took the stairway up to a cafeteria. He paused at a window, watching the chain of gondolas rising toward the white peak, wondering which was hers, who she was, where in the world she had come from. He imagined going after her, stepping out into the snow to find her waiting, arms open for an embrace. Another Linda, this one his. He would never go home. He would spend the rest of his life with her in a place unlike any he had ever imagined. Then he blushed at the foolishness of his fantasy.

•

Out on the deck that circled the cafeteria, people were sunbathing, sprawled in chairs, stretched out on plastic chaise lounges, some wearing only bikinis. A pure white snow dazzled from the surrounding mountains, so brilliant that Mark's eyes ached. He bought cheap sunglasses at a souvenir stand and looked out at a darkened world.

Before he located the path he and Freddy had chosen from a guidebook description of a country neither of them had ever seen, Mark reviewed his hiker's map to get a sense of the turns of the trails and the altitudes ahead. Then he hoisted his backpack high on his shoulders and set out. Arrows on a signpost pointed toward destinations in three directions. The climber's hut where he would spend the night was four hours away. He tried to imagine what it would have been like to start off with Freddy and Linda, having to watch them touch all day, Freddy large and strong and clumsy, stumbling over rocks and roots, Linda looking back at Mark with her sly smile. He had never been able to judge if it were a look of amusement or scorn. What would have happened if he and Linda were ever alone? He imagined furtive groping, she provoking him into a passion that would humiliate him. It was much better to be by himself.

After ten minutes he could take off the sunglasses. The day was still bright, but now the snow was on distant peaks and the trail a mixture of rock and dirt. All at once his boots sank in icy mud; he lost his footing and sprawled on his back, feeling like an idiot, glad no one was around to see. The mud caked in his boots and smeared on his trousers.

He sat on the grass, cleaning his boot treads with jabs of a twig, muttering curses. Then a breeze touched his face like a soft hand, and he paused to take in the panorama spread out before him, towers of ice and rock layered back to the horizon. Across a sheer valley a huge peak pierced the clouds, seeking the sky. For the first time, Mark felt the power of the mountains, the awe of being so close to a massiveness so vast and soaring. He cried out in wonder, then trembled with embarrassment even though he was utterly alone.

•

By late afternoon, the sun still high, Mark paused to check his map and saw that he was halfway to the hut. He heard cowbells and, when he turned past a bend in the hillside, found a dozen tan animals gathered at a stream, some with hooves deep in the icy rush, heads bobbing as they munched grass. He stepped carefully on the path to avoid manure piles.

Across a field a sod-roofed shed stood by the trees, the first building he had seen since the lift, a low ramshackle structure with a thick black door. The sun struck great boulders in the earth beside it and glittered back so brightly Mark had to put on the sunglasses again.

Then he noticed a man at the side of the shed cutting hay on a hillside, bare-chested, small and taut, swinging a scythe with sweeping stokes. Either his face was in shadow or he was bearded; Mark couldn't tell through the dark lenses. He waved, a gesture of one stranger to another, but the man didn't seem to notice him. He debated calling out when he heard a female voice, and there to his amazement from behind the shed stepped the woman from the train, still in the same pink running shorts and brown sleeveless top, though now in heavy boots that came up to mid-calf.

Mark wanted to hide, but he was exposed on the path, fifty yards from any trees. She cupped her hands to her mouth and shouted something he couldn't make out, then signaled with excited gestures, about to rush toward him. He waved and called out, "Great day," pretending that she would be content with just a greeting, then hurried away without looking back.

•

When a sign told him he was nearing the hut, he suddenly stood in the midst of a landscape unlike any he had ever seen, a grassless field of ebony stone and shallow ponds that reflected the stark hillsides. His first sensation was one of bleakness, and then it struck him that he was surrounded by a terrible beauty, beyond any living thing. Despite the warmth of the day, he shivered at being alone in such an inhuman place, then ran across the rocks until he saw a valley of trees ahead.

•

The climber's hut, a stone building hugging a mountainside, turned out to be the size of a small guesthouse, with a shower room and a kitchen that served hot meals. His bed was one of a row in a dormitory-style room for men on the second floor. The first had a similar room for women, the third several small double rooms.

Mark, freshly showered, massaged his aching calves and sprawled out on his bed for an hour before he went down for dinner. A few people looked up at his entrance, couples sitting by themselves in the corners. But long tables filled the room, clusters of men and women shouting conversations in French and German and stranger languages, erupting in laughter.

Mark ate by himself at the last free table, reading his guidebook. Someone asked, in English, if he minded if she joined him. He looked up and there carrying a tray was the woman from the cable car, the woman who was not Linda. "What are you doing here?" He gasped, stunned by her presence.

"Pardon?"

"Don't you remember me?"

She smiled as if he were joking. "Should I?"

"I was looking at you on the cable car. I followed you to the gondola."

"Why would you do that?"

"I thought you were someone else." Mark felt himself getting flustered and saw that several people at the big table next to him had paused to look.

She pulled back a chair and sat at the table, amused, as if they were playing a game. "Who? An old romance?"

Mark blushed at the word. "My friend's fiancée."

"Am I so much like her?"

She spoke English precisely, softly, as one who had learned the language through years of schooling. Now that she was so close, he saw many differences, all the ways she couldn't be Linda. "Not as much as I thought. You're better."

She touched a hand to his sleeve and laughed. "You don't even know me."

"I know her."

"Then I am glad I am not this Linda."

"So am I."

"I am called Monika." She reached across the table to shake his hand, and Mark introduced himself in return.

"Is this a trick you use often?" she said.

"What?"

"Tell young women you would like to meet they are another person?"

You're very lovely, he wanted to say and realized he didn't care who she was. It was very pleasant to watch her smile. Perfect, he thought, absolutely perfect. Until a nightmare image struck him: the woman from the train tripping through the door with her huge pack and heading straight for their table. Why not? Where else would she sleep this night?

But she did not appear, even after the meal when he and Monika sat outside to watch the sun set behind the mountains. She asked why he was here, why he had chosen this place. He tried to explain how it had felt to stop on the trail and look out in disbelief, how he wished someone like her had been with him to share that moment. She listened, smiling, nodding, even though he felt the failure of his words. Yes, it had been that way for her too. He wanted to tell her about the barren landscape too, how terrified he had been, but feared that an admission of cowardice would ruin everything. When they parted, she squeezed his hand and said she would look for him at breakfast.

•

In the morning Mark splashed his face at the sink in the room and stepped to the window, dazzled by the misty glow of sunrise. It was very early and the others, men from the crowded tables, were still sleeping, huddled under blankets in the mountain chill. Mark shivered barefoot and realized how eager he was to see Monika again.

Outside on a hillside a small scruffy man pushed a wheelbarrow piled with stones with one hand and balanced a grey-handled adz over his shoulder with the other. He wore brown dirt-stained trousers and a torn shirt buttoned over a second shirt of Burberry plaid. It struck Mark as odd that a lone worker so far from a village owned such a shirt. An unkempt black beard grew high on his cheekbones. At first Mark thought the man was screwing up his face deliberately, then realized that his expression was permanently distorted. There was something familiar about him. He might have been the man cutting hay back on the hillside yesterday. Strange that he should be here, in another place.

In the dining room he sat at the same table as the night before just drinking coffee, unwilling to serve himself until Monika appeared. He stared at the door, his heart jumping every time someone swung it open to enter. The tables were filling up, but still she did not enter.

Then from outside he heard excited voices, German exclamations, cries from the distance. Chairs scraped back on the stone floor, people suddenly standing and crowding toward the door. Mark stood with them, shook a man's arm. "What is it?"

"Ein Körper."

"What?"

"A body. A corpse."

"Where? Whose?"

"In the rocks. A woman."

Mark rushed out, banging his hip into the edge of a table, spilling hot coffee over his hand and grunting at the sudden pain. His first thought was Monika, that he was being cheated. But there she stood among a group of excited people and gestured for Mark to join them, her face grim, quivering at the edge of tears.

"What happened?" he asked, relieved at her presence. In the bright light of morning, he saw she was nothing like Linda. He didn't know how he ever could have confused her. "What do you know?"

"The early walkers found her. The cows grazing right next to her as if nothing were wrong."

And he finally understood what he should have realized at the first shouts. The woman from the train. The woman who should have joined them in the hut. Last night he had wanted so much to forget she existed.

A middle-aged couple, both thin and sinewy, with tight lined faces, looking more brother and sister than man and wife, stood in the center of the group and told their story. Monika translated for Mark, her mouth close to his ear, the words warm against him.

The couple had started walking when it was still moonlight, when the mountains were nothing but dark shapes, the cows blurred among the rocks. Just as the sun came up above the eastern peaks, something made them both turn around, suddenly and simultaneously, not a sound, just a shared sensation. Together they saw the foot, bare and twisted, protruding between two boulders at the edge of the grass. They ran and found her, a broken body wedged into a mound of grey stone.

Mark tried to envision the scene, the height she had fallen from. Someone spoke the words he was thinking: a terrible accident. But the couple shook their heads, slowly, grimly. Not an accident. A great sharp blow had crushed her forehead. Blood splashed across the rock. Murder. Mark could feel Monika shrink at the word and press against him.

"Was she raped?" he blurted, immediately embarrassed at the attention of the others. Monika gave him a strange look.

The man shrugged. "She had clothes on. But nothing much. Just shorts and a top."

"Only one boot was off," his wife added. "The bare foot."

The man by the shed. He must have been the one, bare-chested yesterday, in the Burberry shirt today. Mark was certain they were the same, for an instant wondering if he were the shepherd from the island, stalking the woman for weeks, driven to avenge his humiliation.

He pulled Monika away from the group. "I know who she is."

"How could you?"

He explained about the train ride, the encounter on the trail. "She wanted to tell me something. He was behind her with a scythe, and I just walked away."

"Was she frightened?"

"She must have been desperate. But I didn't look at her long enough to notice."

"Why didn't you go to her?"

"I wanted to get to the hut and meet you."

"Me! I didn't exist for you."

"I'd been thinking about you all day."

"About someone," she said. "You were lonely."

Mark seized her hand, half expecting her to vanish, leaving him with nothing but a clenched fist.

"We should go away from here too," she said. "Now." She gestured out toward the mountains. "All this beauty. It is being ruined."

He looked back across the valley in the direction of the body and felt a great need. "There's something I have to do for her."

"It's too late to do anything."

"I have to know her name."

"She was a stranger."

"If she had been you, she'd still be alive."

"How do you mean?"

"She's dead because I found her homely and boring."

Monika shook her head. Her eyes told him he was making a great mistake, but he turned away and began moving, faster and faster, stumbling across the rocks, plunging forward.

•

Mark tried to look at nothing as he hurried his passage through the empty landscape, its dreadful barrenness chilling his thoughts. He felt surrounded by monstrous shapes and knew why these peaks once terrified the people who lived among them.

Her body would be twisted and broken. His imagination superimposed the image of what he would find over the great shafts of jagged stone that surrounded him. Naked legs wedged into the angles of the rocks, the pink shorts jarring against the pale grey. Fists clenched, back arched in a wrenching thrust to save her life.

He remembered Linda on the sofa in the split second after he had pulled free from her: sprawled against the cushions, skirt bunched up around her waist, hips twisted, eyes squeezed shut as if in pain. They had never liked each other; there had been a tension whenever they were together. But for an instant he—perhaps both of them—had been mad with desire.

And in the station, at the sight of the woman's tanned legs, he had felt a surge of lust. If he had seen her from no other angle, if they had met in some dark place where he would know her only in shadows, he would have held her, pressed against her through the night as he had longed to possess Monika.

Here, absolutely alone on a path in the mountains, he had the sensation that Monika was merely a fantasy conjured by the intensity of his need. If he returned to the hut and asked the others, shook them by the shoulders to admit the truth, they would say he had eaten alone, had spoken to no one that morning.

Even though Mark had taken this route only once, sights began to feel familiar—a cluster of trees, the angles of the peaks, the shape of the ice in a crevasse. Up ahead he saw the shed sagging against a hillside and knew he was very close. He could make out a cluster of men standing amid the cattle, a few in suits, others in brown uniforms. Officials. They must have been standing over the body, looking down at her; an oversized woman with limbs askew, mouth open, eyes staring, a gaping red gash where her forehead should have been. Much more fascinating dead than she had been alive.

He saw a car parked on the trail, white with a checkered door and a blue dome on the roof. It surprised him that a road gave access to this spot, that someone could get here merely by driving. It had cost him such a great effort.

Mark wedged into a gap in the rocks and, hidden, peered out to watch the officials search for clues. Two men in uniform were kneeling at the edge of a spread of grey stone that reached up into a cleft of the peaks. Two others in suits were standing over them gesturing and pointing. Then Mark noticed her pack on the ground beside their legs. Had she heaved that pack at the murderer, a final gesture before he swung the weapon down from over his head?

Her name must have been inside, on her passport among the clothing, perhaps written into a book or the envelope from a saved letter. She must have a family back home, people who loved her. How awful it would be to love her, how awful to see her like this.

Mark heard a soft puttering sound and looked up to a red helicopter passing along the valley between the highest mountains, nearing until it hovered above the men and he could make out the blur of the rotor blade and two people seated behind the windows. It descended slowly until it was only twenty feet from the ground. The wind flapped the men's clothing as they shouted to the pilot, words that were just a blast of sound to Mark. Some sort of harness dropped down from the helicopter. A uniformed man leaped to catch hold of it. Then Mark could not tell what they were doing. But after several minutes, he saw a dark shape stretched between the braces of the harness lifting from the ground. Her body, sealed in a black bag, hoisted like some inert load, dangling in the air. He would never know who she was.

He should reveal all he knew, emerge from the stone to tell the officials about the bearded man with the scythe, the twisted man with the adz. But he was afraid to expose himself, to have them ask questions he would be ashamed to answer.

The four men stared up as the body was drawn into the helicopter until, with a flap of rotors, it rose above the mountains and disappeared. Then one in uniform carried her pack to the trunk of the car. Another, in a suit, followed with a square case. Now only two lingered at the spot where she had been found. They circled around scanning the ground. One kicked a pebble and watched it tumble downhill. Finally, they joined the others in the car and drove off.

Mark stepped out into the emptiness of the field and then stood frozen. At last, with a shout, as if breaking chains, he rushed directly to the rocks where the body had lain and dropped to his knees, reaching out to the blood-smeared stone, unwilling to touch it, sensing an icy chill beneath his fingertips.

His chest heaved, but he could not cry. Dry and rigid, he knelt, knowing that he would not move from that spot all the day, not until the sun set and brought a fearful darkness; then he would make himself stand and begin his walk back to a place where no one waited.

WALTER CUMMINS has published seven short story collections—*Witness, Where We Live, Local Music, The End of the Circle, The Lost Ones, Habitat: stories of bent realism, Telling Stories: Old and New*. He also has published four collections of essays and reviews—*Knowing Writers* and *Death Cancer Madness and Meaning, Irresponsible and Maladjusted,* and *Seeking Authenticity*.

More than one hundred of his stories, as well as memoirs, essays, and reviews, have appeared in magazines. With Thomas E. Kennedy, he is founding co-publisher of Serving House Books, an imprint for novels, memoirs, and story, poetry, and essay collections. For more than twenty years, he was editor of *The Literary Review*. He is now editor emeritus.

His other publications include *Our Literary Travels* and *The Literary Traveler*, co-written with Thomas E. Kennedy; *Programming Our Lives: Television and American Identity*, co-written with George Gordon; and collaboration on five books about the Vanderbilt-Twombly Florham Estate in New Jersey.

He is a professor of English Emeritus at the Florham Campus of Fairleigh Dickinson University, where he taught in the MFA Program in Creative Writing and the MA Program in Creative Writing and Literature for Educators. His degrees are a BA in English from Rutgers and an MA in Humanities, MFA in Creative Writing, and PhD in English from the University of Iowa.

www.ingramcontent.com/pod-product-compliance
Lightning Source LLC
Chambersburg PA
CBHW030227180626
46810CB00008B/3011